A CROWN OF GLORY

G. LaVerne Crowell

Other Books by G. LaVerne Crowell

ICEX Intelligence, Vietnam's Phoenix Program

Mountain Trials

The Mark of the West

The Roar of War

ISBN: 978-0-6151-4894-6

Crowell Publishing

DEDICATION

For a good friend in Washington, Tim Skidmore

His encouragement led me on

CHAPTER ONE

George Franklin was drafted into the Army. He had no real concern but only intended to serve his country. There were no wars at present and he had been considering joining up anyway. George was 18 years old and had ambitions for the future as most young men did. George trained through an abbreviated basic training and was sent to advanced infantry training. He did very well through all the training and had begun to almost like the Army. George had grown up in a medium sized city of Tucson, Arizona. He currently had no attachment to any girls, but had dated as most boys did during high school. The Army would be his home for at least two years, the standard induction term, and it would feed and clothe him and give him a roof. Things like this were hard to dismiss for a young man. George had made no plans for his future as yet. He had always been in the center of society as far as intelligence and wants. So this was a given space to find out more about him. He had no visions about glory and only wanted to see some of the country. He was assigned to Fort Leavenworth as his first assignment out of training. This was a lot colder than Tucson was in the winter and even most of the summer.

George wanted to see a lot of the area around Fort Leavenworth, but he had no car to use. He was saving some of his pay to be able to purchase an older car before long. George did not drink but smoked. He could purchase cigarettes at the Post Exchange for 50 cents a carton. His new assignment did not have much training time involved just some boring things like guard duty and Kitchen Police. KP was one of the duties that all soldiers hated. You had to work 15 or 16 hours for the day and work most of the time cleaning pots and pans and setting things up for the meal service the rest of the service men needed. Fort Leavenworth had some good points like a movie theater that had top movies at 5 cents each. There was a bowling alley, but George had never learned to bowl. Other minor recreation things were available, but George wanted to get around the area. He had found that a bus would transport anyone with a

CHAPTER ONE

pass off to local civilian places, like downtown Leavenworth. George wrote home about once a week and his parents wrote back about the same. This was George's first time away from home as with most young men here.

One of the guys from George's company was telling him that there was a used car lot just off the post. He had nice looking cars for good prices. But there was no warrantee for the vehicles. George had some money saved up so over the weekend he asked for a pass off base and it was granted. George walked off base and could see the car lot about a half-mile ahead. He walked there and into the yard. A salesman saw him and he stood out like a serviceman due to his dress and haircut. The salesman asked what he was looking for and George told him an older car good for the local area. The salesman took him over to a nice looking 1937 Chevy. It looked clean and sounded good running. George asked how much and the man told him $35. No this would be too much. The salesman asked George how much he could pay. George told him $25. The salesman shook his head, but told George to wait here. He went to talk with the sales manager. When he came back, he told George he had talked the man down to $27 so George said ok. The car was currently licensed so this was the next step that had been already covered. George bought the car and drove off. He wanted to check the car out some and see how it ran. George was feeling very well and enjoyed his run around the area. He stopped and put some gas in the car and drove to the other side of Leavenworth. George felt like a senior in high school again. He was free and happy roaming around. George finally had to return to the post. He needed to register his car with them and find where he could park it. The registration office was along the side of the road opposite the main gate guardhouse. He did the registration and asked about parking. He was told to see his orderly room and they generally assigned parking.

George drove by the mess hall and parked. He was getting hungry so in he went. He was talking to a couple of new friends here and told them about the car. He was proud of his gain. The three talked during their meal and they told George they would like to go for a ride if he was not doing anything this afternoon. So the next adventure was formed. These two had a pass but hadn't decided to walk off the post and get a bus yet. Now George could take them out. They finished their lunch and walked to the car. The three looked the car all over and thought it was in good shape. It was clean and not banged up anyway. They checked the engine and it appeared to be fine. It didn't smoke when you first started it as many cars did. Everyone gave George the well-done nod.

CHAPTER ONE

The three decided to check out some of the countryside around Leavenworth. George did not want to get a long ways from the post until he had more confidence in his vehicle. But they ran a few miles out and enjoyed the land. George was wondering if any places around here held weekend dances. Back home they had Grange Halls in the countryside, which usually held dances at least every two weeks. They would have to ask around. The afternoon was closing toward evening and the three friends headed back toward the post. Someone had said that the post theater had a good movie on tonight. They could get dinner at the mess hall and still have time to get to the movie. So plans were made for now.

The movie was a John Wayne Western so everyone was glad of this. The newsreel at the beginning of the show told various news around the world. Berlin, Germany was holding it's spot daily due to the Berlin Wall that was being constructed and the Russian shutdown of access to West Berlin. No one thought about another war there, but you could really never tell. With the newsreel over and the cartoon finished, the movie began. This was in color, so it was special. George bought a large bag of popcorn for 5 cents and shared with the other two. Today's activity had been enjoyed by the three and after the movie they headed back to the barracks. They had one more day off before they had to get into some work detail. The company they were in was an infantry company but all they did was assigned tasks, most of which were not any fun. George did not go to church here as he figured he had much more important things to do. He enjoyed his personal private life and wanted to do as much as he could without normal civilization activities to bend him into a classic citizen.

Sunday morning came around and George was up, shaved, washed up and headed toward the mess hall for some breakfast. He met his two friends already here. They asked George if he was going traveling today. He was thinking about it and so the two asked to go if he did. Yesterday had been fun and freedom for the guys. George was thinking about cruising a couple small towns in the area. Maybe they could find some girls to travel with. The thought was nice anyway. They drove out to one of the small towns and stopped by a small café. There were kids all around the place, so the three went in and ordered a coke. They were looking things over here and a girl walked up to them and asked where they were from. They were not locals and she knew this. They told her and asked what everyone did around here on a Sunday. She told them you did what you

CHAPTER ONE

wanted more or less as it was hard to get into trouble in a small town like this.

George asked her if she had a couple of friends that might go for a ride with them. She smiled and told the guys to hang on, and she left. The girl came back in a few minutes with two more girls. They all got up and walked over to George' car. The girls selected the boy she wanted to be with and everyone got into the car. George asked where they wanted to go. George introduced Bob and Bill to the girls, and the girl with George introduced her friends as Sandy and Ann. She was Fran. So all the formalities finished, they drove off to somewhere. Fran mentioned a small lake close by that was nice on Sundays. So they drove to it. It was a nice lake and the sun was warm, lending itself to a very nice afternoon. The boys all bought the girls a soda and they sat at park benches overlooking the lake. They had a wonderful time sitting and talking for sometime. Finally, Fran said she needed to get back as her family had a dinner over at another families house for the evening. George drove back into the small town and let the girls off. George asked if they were around the café a lot. Fran pointed to a house in town that was where she lived. She told him to come by anytime he was in town.

A CROWN OF GLORY

The three guys had an enjoyable time this afternoon and could see future things with these girls. They drove off toward the post once again. They had to get ready for the next day. They shinned their boots and checked their brass in case there was a uniform change. For now, the fatigue uniform was the general uniform of the day. George checked his uniform for tomorrow and was ready to get onto duty in the morning. He hit the bed early as he had to be up and running about 5 in the morning. This would be a whole new day to get through and always with unknown situations occurring.

At 5 the next morning, the barracks chief woke everyone and started the new day. First formation on the company street gave early information. Next the company would run for about two miles and return to the mess hall for breakfast. After breakfast, the company held another formation to assign duties for the day. George was assigned guard duty at the ammo dump. This wasn't real bad as there were people around the dump that worked there. The corporal of the guard came around hourly to check on the station and the soldier on duty there. Lunch gave the guard a choice. You could go to the mess hall or you could ask for a sack lunch. George generally asked for the sack lunch. It was always good, with two sandwiches of lunchmeat and

CHAPTER ONE

cheese, a piece of fruit, a bag of chips and a candy bar. A soda was offered with the lunch also. This was much easier than running into the mess hall. George could sit at a picnic table the workers had here and eat his lunch while still on duty.

George rather liked guard duty here, as it was not real boring with other workers around. He could walk around the two bunkers and stretch his muscles. The men talked with him a lot also. His main job was to be here in case someone tried to get to the bunkers to steal some explosives or ammo. The workers would know if the person was not a worker and holler for George. He carried live ammo for his rifle here. The change over for the next guard shift would bring the new guard with the corporal of the guard. The guards exchanged information and then the off duty guard was driven back to the company. The corporal debriefed the off duty guard while in route to the company. Once you arrived at the company, you had to wipe your rifle down, turn it in to the armor sergeant along with the ammo you had signed out. You had to return exact rounds that you had been issued in the morning. With this all finished, you were relieved from duty for the night.

George generally returned to his barracks and polished his boots for the next day. He always checked everything to make sure he was ready for a surprise inspection. If you got gigged during an inspection, you would loose your off base pass privilege for the week. George wanted to keep this now especially as he had his car now. He also had desires to see Fran again. She had impressed him but he was not interested in getting to deep with anyone girl. He was just enjoying the company and whatever else might come around. George usually wrote a note home with a little bit each day and sent once a week. After he was ready for the morning, George walked over to the recreation room for the company. There were two pool tables here, books to read, and a radio. There generally was a local newspaper or two. George kept up with the news somewhat and watched hot spots around the world. He was not real happy about going to war but he was in the Army.

CHAPTER TWO

George's day began as usual. This day he was assigned a new post. He was to fill in for a guard tower at the Army prison here. He thought this might be interesting. He had seen the towers and wondered how this job was. He had an idea it might be fairly boring. Now he would find out for sure. George and the corporal arrived at the main gate to the prison and parked the jeep. They walked inside the main guardhouse at the gate and George reported in. Another corporal took him to a stairway going up the prison wall to the watchtower. Here he relieved the last guard. The corporal told him the basic rules here and left, saying he would be back up in a moment. The tower had a phone in it to call the guardhouse. George looked around and could see fairly well round the inside of the prison yard. As promised, the corporal returned and gave George more information about the duty here. He was required to call in once an hour and more often if he noticed anything that seemed different. The corporal handed George two clips of live ammo for his M-1 rifle. He was told to load one and carry the rifle everywhere he walked to. He could walk the wall top half way to the other guard towers. Lunch would be delivered to him in the sack lunch method. This was fine with him. Two milk half-pints would be delivered with the lunch. Water was available in the tower with a large water bottle.

George was enjoying watching the prisoners in the yard below. They were allowed out of their cell most of the day. A special section of the yard was fenced off for high security prisoners and also one for those on death row. The normal prisoners could play ball or just sit or walk. The day was basically theirs to do in the prison yard. George had been shown the red line just off the wall that prisoners could not cross. There was a booklet in the guard tower also which showed guard information and instructions. George thought it would have been nice to have a radio up here, but he was sure that would not be approved by the guardhouse. George could see that a person could get into daydreaming up here. There was so much to see from up here that he never got close to a daydream. At noon, his lunch was delivered and he could sit in his tower to eat. There was a chair just out from the tower that guards could sit in also. George could imagine this duty would be not so good during bad weather if you had to walk the wall. He had not seen any heating equipment in the tower either.

At four in the afternoon George was relieved from the tower. He had to get down to the guardhouse and turn his ammo in also. Next he would be driven back to his company. All in all, George had enjoyed this day. He told the corporal this also, hoping he might get the duty more often. When he arrived back at the company, he turned his rifle back in and was relieved from duty for the day. He walked to the recreation room and read some of the days news. There was some new information about Korea. The North Koreans were moving down into South Korea and the United Nations was having a fit. George listened to some news on the radio and didn't hear much so he walked to the mess hall. The food here was not always the greatest, but there always was a lot of it. After supper, George walked back to the barracks and prepared for the coming day. He had to send out laundry tomorrow also. He finished this and wrote the addition to his weekly letter and walked back to the recreation room. He played a couple of games of pool and then sat and read some more articles in the local paper. His week moved along in this normal way. On Friday afternoon, George went to the orderly room and asked for a weekend off post pass. He knew of no other duties for him and he was issued the pass. At the mess hall later, George asked Bill and Bob if they were interested in going out to see the girls this weekend. They agreed and so they got off post passes also. The guys agreed to leave the post about noon. They really weren't sure if or when the girls would be available. The three of them walked to the day room and relaxed some. The movie at the post theater did not look that good, so they had decided to relax and get to bed early. Maybe they might need extra energy tomorrow.

Saturday arrived and George arose and did his morning chores before heading to the mess hall for breakfast. After breakfast he walked back to the day room and read a newspaper. He was just waiting until time to go now. his weekends had not been real busy anyway. Sometimes he almost liked getting extra duty to help get rid of the boredom. The girls were fun and what guy didn't like girls anyway. It was much preferable to sitting around with a bunch of other guys on the post. About 11:30, Bill and Bob showed up at the

CHAPTER TWO

day room. They were all ready to go now. They went to the car and drove off toward the small town. They arrived as before and went into the café to purchase a coke. George looked around but did not see any of the girls. They carried their drinks outside and sat on a bench there. They had been sitting here about 10 minutes, when the three girls came walking toward them. They must have been keeping watch for the guys, unless they just decided to walk to the café at this time. They walked up to the guys and said hi. They talked for a time here and George asked if they wanted a soda. They agreed so Bill and George entered the café again and got three more. The bunch now sat out front of the café and talked for a few minutes. Fran finally asked if the guys were going for a ride or out to the lake. George answered that whatever they wanted to do was ok. They jumped into the car again and were off. They did stop by the lake for a while as it was nice on the grass there. They sat and talked for a while, waiting for each other to suggest something else to do. Bob mentioned that none of the guys really knew the country much around here. The girls offered to show them some of it. So they drove around and enjoyed a couple of hours with the girls. Ann mentioned that there was a dance at a local grange hall tonight. Bill said he couldn't dance and Sandy spoke up that she would be happy to teach him. The dance was to begin about 7. They all now drove back to town and the girls left them at the café. They promised to meet them here about 6:30. This was great and the guys were wondering about going back to the post for supper or to get a hamburger here. They finally agreed to get a hamburger here and save time. They would have about an hour and a half to wait, so after eating their hamburgers, they decided to walk around the small town and see the place. It seemed like a very nice quiet place. The town had a small grocery store, a drug store with a soda fountain, a hardware store, a gas station, and a second hand store. A person probably could live in this town and not have to leave very often.

Finally the guys headed back toward the café. There were more young people around the place now. It must have been an evening meeting place. 6:30 came around and so did the girls. They all climbed into the car and headed toward the grange hall. The girls directed George how to get there. They arrived and found quite a few cars parked around the edges of the hall. The person at the door asked for 20 cents per person and the guys paid. They were having a local small band with a piano, a base fiddle, and guitar. The band was tuning up right now. The group found a place to sit and waited for the music to begin. George was really enjoying himself. The girls were chattering like little monkeys and the

CHAPTER TWO

guys just winked at each other. The girls were living high up with their male escorts. The girls had told them they were all around 17. The boys were about 19, so all in all the ages were good. The girls were in their last year in high school. They had talked as girls do, with friends and told them about the Army guys they had caught.

The hall was getting crowded now and the band looked ready to go. They had a mike so they could talk to everyone and they now welcomed everybody to the hall and the dance. With this, they struck up a tune. The dance floor reached half full very fast. Fran drug George out and the other girls had done the same with the other two guys. Fran was a good dancer and George had danced a lot in high school, so they got along very well. Sandy and Bill were also getting along as Sandy was showing Bill some things. Bob and Ann were getting along like George and Fran were. The dance ran on and the fun was getting better. George did notice some of the men were getting wobblier on the dance floor. Fran laughed and admitted that many of the men came here more to drink around their cars than to dance. She asked George if he had anything to drink. Unfortunately he had nothing. She told him to bring something next time and they would have some fun. George was not sure what she was saying but had some vivid mental pictures. The dance was finally slowing down and was close to ending. People were leaving now and the floor was getting less used. George asked if the others wanted to stay or leave. They didn't care so whatever happened would be fine. Fran suggested that they leave and maybe we could stop at a place she knew about. So the six-man crew got in the car and drove on. They were about to town when Fran told George to turn at a crossroads. He did and she guided him to a small road the sort of looked over the town from a few feet up. George noticed more cars here and he got the idea.

George pulled up in a place overlooking the town below and viewed a very pleasant sight. Things were just beautiful all around and the evening was cooler. He turned off the motor and Fran snuggled close to him. They were talking softly and probably not hearing anyway. George was not unskilled in these kind of spots but had been somewhat confused by Fran's suggestion after he found out what was going on. The couples in the back were busy and not talking very much. George was enjoying having Fran here with him. As time went on and activities began to gain, Fran told George they had to be home by midnight. George looked at his watch and found they should be leaving about now. So he warned the other couples and started the car. They backed out and drove toward town. This had been quite an evening

CHAPTER TWO

out. The girls got out at the café and gave their partner a last kiss and left. The guys just sat here for a few minutes. Sandy came running back and asked if they were coming out tomorrow. They all said yes, so she smiled and ran back. George started the car and headed back to the post. The guys talked all the way back.   None of them had ever seen such a rush job as they just had. Bill wondered if maybe they should get some blankets and put them in the trunk. None of them had ever seen such fast work by girls. They really didn't seem like these type of girls either. They drove back to post talking about all this. George told them he really wasn't thinking of anything permanent right now.

They would have to see how things went in the near future. Playtime was wonderful, but most of the time there was a big string attached. None of the guys could afford a marriage at this time. They arrived at the post and headed to their barracks.   They might still need a lot of rest for tomorrow.

A CROWN OF GLORY

CHAPTER THREE

Morning came and George dressed and headed to the mess hall. He had been thinking of how he could get some booze, but no plan was coming along. He could buy beer on post, but not anything else. Maybe he could make friends with a NCO who was allowed to purchase whiskey. Of course, he had to watch his money as the pay was very thin yet. The guys didn't drive out to the town until later. Today being Sunday, maybe the girls had to go to church and generally such did not end until noon. So they planned to arrive in town about 1. They all sat around in the day room now talking and wondering what today might bring. Bill had obtained a couple of blankets and George put them in the trunk. They all figured to head out to the town and see what the day held. You really could never tell. The guys pulled into the café parking lot and found a lot of people around today. The girls were already here and each ran up and planted a big kiss on their man. After this, everyone climbed into the car and George drove off. The guys were confused now as to how the girls were acting.

Fran told George they wanted to go to another lake not far if that was ok with him. Everyone felt this was fine, so Fran told him how to get there. George drove on and Fran would advise him on junctions until they arrived at the lake. This one was larger than the other one, but it was pretty also. Fran told George where to park and the day was just perfect. The couples walked down toward the lake and each girl had her man held by her arm. The girls were just like yesterday, chatting all the time. This lake had a nice beach on it and when they had walked here, the girls started skipping stones over the water. The sand here was white and very fine. It must have been brought in George thought. Everyone decided to take their shoes off now and walk in the sand. This was a funny and nice feeling all at once. There were a couple of people on the other side of the lake, but no one could be seen on this side. Ann suggested everyone should go for a swim as the lake looked so nice. The guys said they had not brought any swimsuits. The girls said they hadn't either.

CHAPTER THREE

Last one in was a rotten egg! The guys were amazed as the girls stripped down and walked in the water. Well this could be fun the guys thought, so they shucked down also and entered the lake. Bob did ask about anyone coming here before they got out. The girls told them not to worry. No one ever came here on a Sunday.

Everyone was splashing around and having water fun. The girls would swim up to the guys and brush against them and then leave again. This was getting very difficult for the guys. Every time the girls came up and brushed the guys, things got worse. It was questioned what the guys were thinking by now. They were showing full strength and the girls were having a ball. The girls continued playing and finally came up and hugged the guys. This was as far as they would allow things to go. The guys were in trouble from the teasing girls. Finally, everyone got out of the water and dried off and put clothes back on. The girls told them that today was just to keep them interested. They really snuggled up to the guys now however. The guys were not bitching however, as things were running very fast anyway. They each had questions but they would talk about things later. Everyone agreed to go back to the café and call this day ended. The guys needed to get things ready for duty in the morning. Each couple exchanged telephone numbers and the guys told them their phone numbers were to the orderly room where a message could be left. The girls wanted the guys back next weekend and they agreed if they didn't have extra duty. The girls got out and walked toward their homes. The guys sat for a few minutes trying to figure things out. A high school kid came to their car and introduced himself. He had lived here most of his life, as had the girls. He told the guys they must be something special. These three girls had been reclusive and almost never went out with anyone from the high school. They were considered party poopers at the school. Since they were so very good looking, guys continually tried to take them out, but they were also known as an icy date. This was amusing to the guys now. They told the student they had just met the girls and enjoyed being with them. The student walked away, shaking his head.

The guys were now totally up heaved. This would have never been their opinion of these girls. Now they had no idea what was in the planning by the girls. Things sure seemed different. Nice girls like the student had told them, just did not generally go around acting like these had with them. This whole thing had covered what normally would have taken months, and this in only two weekends. The guys drove back to post and talked about things during the trip. They figured they would just have to see where things were

CHAPTER THREE

going. They arrived back at the post and each went to their barracks. Uniforms had to be readied and boots needed to be shined. When George finished preparing his uniforms for the next day, he walked to the day room. He sat with some friends and talked with them about the girls. He was really lost as yet. The other guys had no idea what was going on either. They all volunteered to step in if George needed some break time from them. George finally walked back to his barracks and crawled in bed.

The coming week ran much like the last ones. George drew KP for Wednesday and he was so happy. This was the worst duty any soldier could draw, at least of anything known. It happened about once a month, and weekends were not kept out from the normal duty roster. George had been reading the news more now as the conflict in Korea was growing rapidly. North Korea was aligned with China, and neither were listening to the United Nations. The United Nations Security Counsel had been meeting daily now and in session for long hours. Lines were being divided between the East and the West. George was afraid that he could be going over there before long. Infantry soldiers usually were the first transferred into a combat area. If the UN decided to go in on a Policing Action, this would be immediate for many infantry units in the states. So George just continued to watch and read all he could about this action. Standard procedure for military units to be transferred was they would be notified at least a month prior to being sent. The Post began calling alerts at all times to test the readiness of the units here. You just had to wait and play the game. George had been wondering what it would be like over there. They had been taught that the modern Army was far ahead of the units in W W II. Soldiers clothing had been much improved as with most of their gear now. George wondered if maybe some of this was just military bull.

The week passed by fast and suddenly it was Saturday again. George asked for a off post pass for the weekend. The clerk was not sure anymore, so he asked the First Sergeant. He came out and talked with George for a minute. He told George to call in to the orderly room three times a day. George got the pass, and the First Sergeant smirked and winked at George. Evidently he had heard things also. The actions of the three soldiers must be all around the base by now. Bob was not given a pass as he had extra duty on Saturday. He could come out on Sunday however. He had called Ann and told her. She was disappointed but there was nothing he could do about it. George and Bill drove out to the town. The girls were waiting for them at the café. It seemed at least half the town was here also. Fran gave

CHAPTER THREE

George a big kiss and pulled him over to the edge of the crowd. She introduced him to her parents and they were glad to met George. Her dad had spent 25 years in the Army and was now retired. He had retired at the top, Master Sergeant E-7. He had been infantry also and came through WWII in one piece. He told the kids to go and have fun. George and Fran got into the car and she slid over next to him. All this and right in front of not only most of the town but her parents also. The same basic thing with Bill and Sandy. It was almost like a plan.

The four of them headed out toward the small lake and Fran was telling George about her father. He had came out of WWII as a very highly decorated soldier. All her life she had heard him tell her to look for a good serviceman to get involved with. These men were stable and would provide not only a good life for her, but they were paid alright too. George was maybe beginning to see something ahead in the plan now. As it turned out, all three girls had fathers who had been in the Army and they had been stationed together overseas. The families mostly stayed here in this town as it was very convenient to the post. The four arrived at the small lake and walked down toward the lake and sat in the grass. George had his arm around Fran and kissed her. Then he asked her if her parents had given her a plan to follow with them. She looked funny for a minute and then she admitted they had a little bit. It seems retired soldiers were deadlining the three soldiers. Fran eyes told him they had been helping her with her man net. He thought this was sort of funny. The guys talked with the girls for a time tending to mostly talk about minor things. But George was thinking about other things now.

George asked Fran to come with him for a minute. As she stood up, her grabbed her and held her tight. Next he kissed her very tenderly and walked a ways with her. She now was curious now more than ever. He told her she needed to know some things. She felt afraid now that maybe he already had a girl or even a wife he had never mentioned. George set her down on the grass and sat tight next to her. He needed to get this out now before things went any further. He asked her if she had been hearing the news about Korea. She said her parents talked about it some. Well George now told her that he was infantry just like her father had been. He would be on a transfer slate almost as soon as anything happened over there. He asked her if she remembered when her father was over seas in the last war. She did and this had her thinking in some past days. George did not think it was right to have her waiting over here if he was over there. She would be throwing a better part of her life away, hoping

CHAPTER THREE

someone over there would return. She was almost in tears now and George held her tightly. He was not dropping her but she needed to do some thinking and talk with her parents about things. George told her he was in a funny state also. He had no intention of getting involved with a girl as yet, but she had just bowled him over. The two of them must have sat there for over an hour and with very few words. They were just letting their minds mix with this closeness and enjoyed the warmth of each other. Finally Fran asked George if they could continue the day and have some fun and enjoy the world. He agreed. She told him she would talk with her parents tonight and she could pass this on to him tomorrow. He agreed and hoped he was able to come out tomorrow. If not he would try to call her. Fran mentioned that they needed to carry on this day as if they never had this conversation. Otherwise, the day would end up a flop. George agreed with this. Fran was wondering if Bill was talking with Sandy about this same thing.

George and Fran came walking back to the other two and tried to act as if nothing was happening. Sandy looked at them and made the move. She said Fran looked as bad as she did probably. What was funny, George and Bill had not discussed talking with the girls about this and now they were. George and Fran laughed and sat down with them. They had decided to enjoy the rest of the day and talk with parents this evening. Sandy told them she and Bill had come to this conclusion also. They laughed and started everything off well, each hugging and squeezing each other. Fran told everyone she had never felt like this before. Sandy admitted the same. The three girls had been hands off girls totally in the past. They had gained a massive amount of hardly acceptable actions with these guys. Each of their dad's had instructed them to go out for what they wanted and leave no negative thoughts. The three guys had not been interested in an attachment to a single girl, but now things had totally changed. The guys all knew what risks they would be in if a war started again. The girl's parents would know this also. So every one of the three girls needed to sit down with parents. Before long, the four had passed the heavy discussion and now were working on a kissing agenda. They managed to enjoy the rest of the afternoon and soon were heading back to town. They would meet the girls again tomorrow unless they called.

CHAPTER FOUR

George and Bill drove back to the post and talked all the way. Their problem was the same. They had been sucked into this situation with their eyes wide open. Everything was now coming together, except this final step that the girls had to accept or rule out. Neither of the two had ever wanted this to go so far, and they did not know that it hid within them. Life is a funny story at times. So now the ball was in the girls court. They both knew what they hoped, but also knew what was fair for the girls. They wondered what Bob would be thinking about this. They had to advise him of the afternoon, as they were sure the girls would do with Ann. George and Bill arrived back at the post and checked with Bob's barracks for him. He was not here, so they walked to the day room. They found him there and told him they needed to speak with him about serious things. The three walked outside and sat at a picnic table out from the day room. Now George and Bill began on Bob. George went first about the wonder they had about the girls' actions in the past. He told them about meeting the girls' parents and later talking with the girls. They had not spoke with Ann however, so this would be up to Bob. He had been thinking along the same lines as George and Bill. He figured to go with them tomorrow and meet with Ann and give the same information if she didn't have it already. So they all needed to wait for morning. Bob had admitted to himself that he was in love with Ann also. This whole thing had tipped the apple cart over as the saying went. It was amusing that three guys just looking for fun, could get involved with girls this fast. The whole thing was geared to the plan that the girls had.

The guys all headed to bed and waited for the morning. Sleep was not involved with the guys at this night's period. They each tossed and turned most of the night. By morning, they all were fairly well worn out. They grabbed breakfast and drove out toward the small town. They arrived at the café and figured they would have a wait on now. They had arrived around 9, so they didn't think there would be

CHAPTER FOUR

anyone around until after church. But they couldn't just sit
at the barracks and go slowly crazy. They had no idea what
they would do if the girls agreed with them to not get this
relationship going further. They all three were almost basket
cases after they sat about 10 minutes at the café parking lot.
Another five minutes passed and then the girls were seen
running toward the car. The guys got out and when the girls
arrived, they grabbed their man and hugged him and planted
many kisses on them. This was different also. Next, Fran
spoke with George. She told him she had some bad news for
him. His head fell down and she told him he was not getting
rid of her this easy. This shocked George and he yelled. The
girls wanted to go to the small lake first. So George drove out
there. They all got out and walked in the grass a ways. They
sat down just apart from each other couple. Fran told
George she had talked with her parents, and they had been
overly impressed that George would have brought this up.
Yes, they knew the risks of everyone's future, but this could
be anywhere. The secret to life and love was to live
everything for the day and hope for the best tomorrow. All
the parents had given the bright green light for the three
soldiers. Fran had told her parents exactly what had gone on
with the guys from day one. This embarrassed the guys, but
it was sanctioned by the parents with smiles. Their dad's had

told them he was glad his wife hadn't acted like this! They had all felt very sorry for the guys. They also hoped the girls would be able to make up for this horrid act. Of course they had all laughed.

There now was a new hitch in any plans. The Army generally did not allow lower enlisted men to get married without special circumstances. Fran's dad had won the Congressional Medal of Honor in WWII against Germany. With this information, he had gained some high respect with higher officers at Leavenworth. He could check with them and see if anything might be possible for this in the near future. Another way was if the girl was pregnant. This was an automatic ok for a marriage. But with this many men were not allowed to live off base with their wives. The guys could not believe the parents of these girls were so strong for this union between them all. This did not happen in this day and age. Before long, the three couples were hard to find as individuals. They all were involved in some heavy smooching in the grass. These girls were definitely not holding up their reputations for being cold. Things had not gone all the way as yet but everyone was very involved in each other. As evening was drawing nearer, the group drove back to town. The girls told the guys there was another grange dance next Saturday and they hoped the guys could come. They next

CHAPTER FOUR

had a request from the parents. They wanted a Bar-B-Cue in the city park Sunday afternoon if possible. This all was fine with the guys. The girls were released finally to go home. The guys would let them know if next weekend was open.

The guys drove back to post and checked in. They went to bed, tired from the day. They did manage to get their things ready for morning before they passed out. Morning came and new details were assigned. Nothing was out of the ordinary. The three men worked their details and returned in the evening for supper. They met in the mess hall and talked again. The three of them were still worn from this last weekend. They hoped they would be free for next weekend. They finally returned to their barracks and performed their duties for the next day. The next day arrived and duty assignments were made. The three men again did the general routine. This evening, they ate supper and sat out in the company park area. It was a very nice night, but it would be cooling down before long. Late fall was coming. They discussed the situation they had once again, and the three were ready for whatever fell toward them. The next day came around again and still no news about any transfers for them. They went to their assigned duties, not thinking about much else. In the afternoon, the three of them were called to the orderly room and picked up from their posts. They arrived at the orderly room and was asked to wait for the CO. When the CO had his current business finished, he came out and called all three men into his office. They walked in and stood at attention until he gave them at ease. He asked the men to sit down. He looked at each one of the men and shook his head. This was not looking good to the men. He now talked and told them he did not know who they knew but the post commander had asked the CO to allow them to get married even thought they were low ranking. The CO also had been asked to be very liberal with weekend passes off post for the three of them. The three soldiers apologized to the CO and told him they had no information about any of this. It was true they had fiancés in a small town close to the base, but had asked no one for any favors. The CO asked about the girls. They informed the CO that they were fantastic girls and they had the best reputations available. The CO suddenly got a funny look on his face. He asked if the girls lived in the small town, which he named. They agreed. Next he asked if one of the girls was named Fran. He gave her last name. This also was true. OK, he had it figured out now. Fran's father was a CMH holder. This was true also. The CO knew her dad and he was a very influential man with the military. George told the CO he was sorry and that he had never asked for anything from this man. The CO

CHAPTER FOUR

agreed and told George if he had asked, the man would have turned him down. Fran's father knew all about the infantry and also knew what George might head into. The Korea thing was shaping up badly. Her father had always upheld his daughter on a very high pedestal. She had always been the most precious thing he had, other than his wife anyway. Now George was beginning to see some things. The CO now talked man to man with the soldiers. He was extremely happy about their chosen women, and would assist in any way he could. If the company did get orders to Korea, he could do nothing about this, but otherwise he would assist them as he could. He thanked the men and dismissed them. He ordered the company clerk to issue them permanent off post passes for off duty times. He now gave the men the rest of the week off.

The three walked out of the orderly room with a wonderful mind toward their girls. They were free now for what ever happened. They jumped in George's car and drove to the town. George drove right to Fran's house and ran to the door. Fran answered and George grabbed her and hugged her. She knew what he was doing. She had been informed that her father had pulled some strings and moved things into George and Fran's court. Fran was overly excited about everything. She had already started some plans. She thought they could get married by a fast justice of the peace for now and plan a regular wedding later. George told her he could not afford a rented house or much else right now. She agreed with him and she told him that her parents had asked them to move into their house for now. They knew what money was and what George was making. If they wanted, there was a bedroom down in the basement that they could work up. There was also a bathroom down there, so they would be fixed fairly well. Now George saw the reason for the off work pass he and the other guys had received. Fran asked him in and he stepped out to tell the others to go to their girl's places. Fran told him to wait, as they all were suppose to meet here. George stepped out and called the other guys in. Things were running fast now. Fran took George down to the basement and showed him the room down there. They would eat with her parents for now. George saw the place and it was a wonderful first room for them. The other girls and their parents were arriving now. Before long there was a big counsel going on here. Evidently, the parents had planned the immediate wedding with a Justice of the Peace, and future big one. Each parent had prepared a room for the newly weds and they could live here as long as they were in the states. The guys were looking at all the planning that had gone on here, and they were amazed. This was a perfect situation planned just for each of them. If they went to war, the girls could still be home and depend upon their parents for help through the vacant periods of their early marriage. The girls with the parents help had planned an early wedding for Friday. The guys had off duty passes for the period of one week to get everything up and running in a marriage.

All the families sat around the living room at Fran's parents and discussed their plans. Things were going very fast for the men, but everything needed to be finished before the guys were sent off to war. The three fathers here knew what lay ahead for the couples. They had never faltered in their quest when they were sent to war and they were very happy to have what they had to help get them through the bad times. The parents were very proud of the men who their daughters had chosen. This was a remake of them selves years behind and they wanted the best that was available for the new grooms. The young couples sat on the couch and loveseat in the living room, arm in arm. The parents could remember this when they were younger. This first marriage coming up would not need best men or the like. Only a couple of witnesses were required. Rings would be obtained by the parents and the guys could pay for them on time at reasonable months payments. This was fine since the soldiers did not have very much money at this stage of the Army game. Fran's father told them not to worry, as they would move up rapidly in rank now. The guys were thinking they needed to get back to post for the night, but arrangements had already been made for them. They would stay in a friend's house in the town that was vacant right now. So as the night ended, the guys said goodbye and thanked everyone for the reception they just had. The night was not quite over as the girls had to show the guys the house they were to stay in. The men were taken to a house and shown the inside. This was a palace almost. The girls locked the doors and took their men into bedrooms here. This was to be a practice honeymoon. The night began to look much better as things continued on. The girls had planned this night with very detailed minor details. There was very little sleep this night for the couples. They did manage to talk a lot however, and they began thinking like they were already moved into their own house. They all knew the dangers they had ahead and the separation of the couples would be hard. The fathers had known this also, but their look was that what ever you had would be moments for eternity.

During WWII, the average soldier would lead girls along with the idea that they probably would never return from the war, and they needed a last wonderful night before

CHAPTER FOUR

heading overseas. Many girls fell into this trap and they worked hard to continue this for every soldier they found. These girls had various names, but they were almost looked upon by soldiers as saviors. The girls here were not captive of anything like this. They had selected their mates for life, regardless how long this might be. And so the night went on.

A CROWN OF GLORY

CHAPTER FIVE

The morning found the couples sitting and talking yet. This might surprise the parents, but the talking was the main thing going on between the couples. With the daylight, they all climbed out of their various beds and got ready to welcome the new day. As for the lack of sleep, the couples felt better than they had for years. The parents had given strict demands that the couples meet them at the café for breakfast. So they did. This was easier than each parent trying to make breakfast for each couple. The parents all asked how last night went they were surprised when they all answered that the main detail of the night was talking for hours. Of course this helped the parents know their son-in-laws to be were the right choice for their darling daughters. Everyone was chatting now and the girls were talking a string of gibberish. Some local residents came into the café and either had breakfast or just coffee and maybe a roll. They all eyed the couples and everyone was sure the whole town was watching them now. George was thinking that last night must have struck terror into some of these old righteous people. The girls were going to miss school today and tomorrow. The parents were insisting that they all finish their high school program at the least.

The guys laughed, wondering what rumors would be running around the school by now. George remembered what the one kid had told him about the girls and how no one could understand what had happen to them. Next Monday would be a whole new era for the school. Here they would have the three icy girls married. The guys called into the post as they had been asked to do. They were advised that as of yesterday, they had been promoted to the rank of Private First Class. This led them through the private ranking and would give them views toward becoming a corporal. Under certain conditions, corporals could get post housing if there were any available. The guys had no idea what plans were made for this day, so they just coasted along, ready for what every might come. The day was more or less a slow one, to allow everyone to relax for Friday. Fran's parents had arranged to meet with a Justice of the Peace in Leavenworth

CHAPTER FIVE

tomorrow. The couples had to get blood tests and normally this took three days, but the family doctor had agreed to do the tests and have the results the next morning. Licenses were obtained also from the county courthouse. Things were running full out and the guys had never dreamed so much was required. It was a good thing they hadn't decided to elope. George could see this would have been a total disaster.

The girls were bubbling around, they were totally happy right now. They were going to get everything they could with their marriage and hope for the best in the future for the guys. This the fathers had stressed fully. You had to live for today and not worry about tomorrow. Even the guys were beginning to see how things ran with the husband in the military. Finally the girls suggested they go for a drive, maybe out to the small lake again. The parents smiled and everyone headed out. The lake had no one around this time of the day. Weekends were the busiest and even then not many people came here. George got the blankets from his trunk and two couples could have these. George and Fran elected to sit at a picnic table. They were into the silent mood again, just holding each other and thinking of futures. The afternoon was beautiful with no clouds, and not too hot or cold. The couples were heading full throttle toward their futures and no one stopped to consider the future. As the fathers had told them, live whole for today and let tomorrow bring what it had. They had told the couples that even bad news could generally be turned around to become helpful. Many people probably would look at this attitude as slip shod and having no intelligent thinking involved. But with an occupation in the service, sometimes this was the way to get through things.

Finally the afternoon was edging closer to evening so everyone decided to head back to town and have a Bar-B-Cue at Fran's parents place. They had a couple picnic tables in their back yard and it didn't take very long to get things up and running for supper. The guys were planning for the next morning. They needed to get their uniforms over to the PX and get the new strips sewed on them. So they would drive to the post in the early morning to start this. They could pick the uniforms up the next day. Tonight's sleeping arraignment was basically the same as last nights. The house was handy and they probably would use it until they had figured out arrangements in the homes of the parents. Plans also needed to be made for weeknights. The guys did not know if it was going to cause any trouble staying out here during the weeknights or not. The fathers were not sure either. The guys probably needed to talk with the First Sergeant regarding this. Everyone sat in the backyard and

CHAPTER FIVE

talked late into the evening. This was good as it gave the parents time to really get to know their new son-in-laws. Finally, everyone began to slow down and it was decided to get some rest for the coming day. The parents all told the kids to get rest tonight and not stay up all night talking. There would be plenty of time for conversation later.

The couples headed for the borrowed house and the parents went to their homes. It was funny now, but all the guys felt relaxed with the girls now. They had reached the stage that they had been going together for years. For one thing, all the talking they had done was a real good platform for these relationships. You never heard of people generally getting married in such a short time. None of the parties involved had any questions about this however. This all seemed as a normal progression toward a life style for each of them. The main thing was that every one of them were the happiest they had ever been and each was totally involved with their partner. The couples did get some sleep this night so they awoke in the morning refreshed. Once again they all headed toward the café for breakfast. The parents could see that everyone had rested this last night and they were glad. It would really be embarrassing to fall asleep during your wedding ceremony. The guys left right after breakfast to get their uniforms and take them to the PX. Fran's father drove into Leavenworth and obtained the blood tests results and also got the marriage licenses for each couple. After these morning runs, the guys returned and they had grabbed their best civilian clothes for now. None of them had suits, but this would wait until the real fancy weddings in the future. The parents were busy arranging various things around this town and Leavenworth. The mothers had arranged for motel rooms in Leavenworth for tonight. This was a small wedding present to the couples. So finally everything was set for this afternoon. Everyone loaded up in cars and they drove back to Leavenworth and met at the Justice of the Peace's office. The arrangement was to perform all three weddings at once. This saved time and money for everyone. The rules were checked and it was found the parents could be witnesses for the weddings.

At the appointed hour, they were ushered into the courtroom. The Justice entered and the ceremonies were under way. The whole things went fast and suddenly the couples were married. The girls were riding very high and the parents were happy. Everyone was gathered together and the court clerk took a picture of the group. They would send the photos out to each of them in about a week. The Justice signed the marriage licenses and gave these to the couples. Now the group drove to a restaurant in town and ate lunch, a

CHAPTER FIVE

bit late. The parents were concerned that the couples might not eat much the rest of the day. The guys had checked about getting the girls their military ID cards. They had been told the Provost Marshal's office would be open until noon on Saturday. So they could take care of this in the morning. The guys had to get their uniforms out of the PX tomorrow anyway. Now there were no unforeseen problems coming the rest of the day. The couples were taken to the motel that had been arranged for them. This was a nice touch for the kids. They had been thinking of staying back at the borrowed house but this was wonderful. Fran's father told them he would be working on the basement room to help them move in before very long. The other girls would have a room in the parents' house also.

The parents now told the kids goodbye. They would see them tomorrow. The couples retired to their rooms and prepared for a wonderful first day of marriage. Fran was thinking about what the school friends were going to say Monday. She was sure there would be many rumors and stories floating around in short order. Everyone would be sure the girls were all pregnant. Actually Fran wished she were pregnant. George and Fran still were talking along with everything else. To say the least, the couples had a wild and full night of everything. By morning, everyone was worn out.

They rested in their rooms until about 9 and then began moving about. They would put their overnight items in the trunk of the car and drive out to the post.

The first stop was at the Provost Marshal to get the girls ID cards. They each still had cards from their fathers, but now this would be from their new husbands. The cards were good for shopping in the PX or the commissary. The ID cards were issued and they next drove to the PX to get the uniforms out. They got these and took them to their barracks. Each soldier carried certain things back with them keep at their new residence places. George took a set of fatigues and one dress uniform. After they had put their uniforms away, they took their new wives to the orderly room to introduce to who ever were there. The CO was here right now and he came out and walked to Fran and hugged her. He told them all they had some good soldiers as husbands and wished them the best for the future. The CO asked Fran about her dad and how he was doing. George had not thought before, but now he could see that Fran's dad was a very well known man.

The guys thanked the CO for everything and bid everyone good day. They drove out toward the small town now. They arrived at Fran's house and walked up the sidewalk. Her parents came out and hugged her and George

CHAPTER FIVE

and invited them inside. They all sat around and talked for a time. After a while, Fran wanted to walk down to the café and see if any friends were there. George could foresee that she wanted to brag some now, so he followed her out of the house. They walked toward the café and met with Ann and Bob who were walking with Bill and Sandy. The whole crowd was here now. They walked into the café and ordered a coke. There were friends in here and of course things instantly began. Everyone began crowding around and looking at the girls' rings. They couldn't believe the girls were really married. The girls introduced their new husbands and the crowd was really growing. Before long, the girls thought it would be better to move outside. The six sat on a bench and other kids crowded around. A couple of girls got almost personal asking the others why they had married so soon. They were curious of certain things. The new wives told them their husbands were in the Army and might have to be sent to Korea, so they wanted in on their lives as soon as possible.

This had ended some of the questions for right now, but the girls knew there would be rumors flowing like wine at a party. It would not take long before the small town had all the information and more about the newlyweds. The poor girls would be faced with good and bad accusations. They did not care, as they were so happy they couldn't even sit still. Their new life was just beginning. They had their man and would do as they needed to. It was the old tale – stand by your man. The couples were beginning young, but this had happened a lot over the years. At least the husbands were getting some money. The three girls had planned on getting some work when they were out of high school. Of course this would be determined if they didn't get pregnant. For now, things would run on and due to the parents insistence, they would more or less support the newly weds for a while.

CHAPTER SIX

Tonight, the couples had agreed to attend the grange dance once again. This didn't cost much and was fun. The girls had desires to show off their catches of course. Around 6:30, the group drove out toward the grange hall. They arrived and parked along side other vehicles and entered the hall. They paid at the door as before. They found a bench and sat down. People started stopping by to greet the girls. The girls got into their pride and joy. They were introducing everyone to their new husbands. There were a lot of shocked faces when this was out. The questions had begun also. Many girls were whispering and asking if the girls had to get married. They would only smile and tell them no. George and Bill walked out to the bathroom outside and a couple of guys spoke with them. They didn't know what these guys had, but the girls had a hard reputation of being the coldest girls in school. And now these guys had come around and got them married in a very short time. The two guys shook their heads and wished them the best of luck. George and Bill just laughed and continued. This would be a very hot topic around the school and town for some time they felt.

The newlyweds danced and had a blast at the grange. The place was fairly crowded tonight and the floor was almost impossible to get on. The band was the same as before. They had played about 5 songs when someone walked up to them and talked for a minute. The leader of the group took the microphone and asked for the attention of the crowd. He wanted to introduce some new people who had just become married. He called the girls and guys up to the front so everyone could see them. Those at the dance that had not heard this before were getting it now. The girls blushed and the guys just stood there. The bandleader thanked them and congratulated the couples. The three couples returned to their bench. The band played on and after a few short intermissions the time came close to 10. The band played until 10:30 as the crowd was wanting. Then it was finished. The newlyweds returned to the various

CHAPTER SIX

accommodations and settled down for the night. The Bar-B-Cue in the town park was still on and a few more people had been invited. So tomorrow would be the end of the week for the newlyweds and a back to normal duty for the coming week. The couples did not bother to stop by the lover's lane where they had stopped two weeks ago after the dance. They each had their own lover's lane now. The kids did not bother to get around until about 8 the next morning.

Fran's mother had fixed some breakfast for them when they came up from the basement. Fran told her parents about the dance and how everyone seemed to know by now. This was a small town, and there was not much that could be hidden. After eating breakfast, George and Fran decided to take a walk around town. The town had some apartments, but Fran did not know how much they were, or what shape they were in. She could check on this during the coming week. She was thinking that maybe they could stay with her parents and just pay them some rent as they could. This would help them for now. And if George had to go to Korea, then she would still be with her family here. This all sounded good and George knew that her parents had offered the room for as long as they needed it. George was thinking his pay should be up to about $50 a month now with his promotion and being married. It might even go higher. At any rate, things would be nip and tuck for a while. George and Fran's dad went outside and sat in the back yard. George wanted to ask him some things about combat. He would like to get any pointers about staying alive. So they talked for a while. George of course knew absolutely nothing about war except what the Army had feed them. Soon Fran came dancing out so this ended their conversation real fast. Fran's mother had made up some snack items for the picnic. Each family was bringing one or two chickens already cooked and mainly just ordinary good food. Fran had made a large bottle of iced tea.

When the time came for going to the park, George helped carry things out to the car. They drove to the town park and met a lot of people here. George was thinking half the town must be here now. So everyone started talking to each other and it was beginning to be a noisy affair. Now a surprise came around, that even the parents didn't know about. The town's people had brought wedding gifts for the couples and they had three tables fixed, one for each couple. This was almost unheard of. They each were given very useful things like towels, sheets, blankets, kitchenwares and various other gifts. The girls were embarrassed and thankful to everyone at the same time. This had been totally unexpected. Now Fran's Father stood up and address the crowd. He thanked everyone for coming and for the gifts. He told the crowd that these marriages were not coming from a 'have to' situation. The parents had pushed their daughters into this as they knew how they felt. He explained that these young men might be leaving soon for a combat assignment in Korea and they wanted their daughters to have some happy moments before this came. Each of the fathers had been through the same situations and they were very glad their wives had been behind them in support. The men in combat needed a thought of something warm and loving back home and the girls needed to share some moments with the men they loved so they might carry these moments through life with them, if anything bad happened overseas. When Ted, Fran's dad, ended his speech, the crowd roared with approval. Now everyone came around once again to congratulate the couples. The picnic lasted almost to evening time and everyone had a very good time. Ted's words were still soaking into various people and they wondered about their sons and daughters. Ted had shown the whole community to meet danger with cheerful reaction.

The guys now helped get everything back into the cars to carry home. There wasn't much food left, but there had been plenty for everyone. At home, the girls began washing various dishes and plates from the picnic and George and Ted sat in the living room. George thanked Ted for his words at the picnic. Ted told him this was all true. He had seen his daughter as she never had been. She was shining love from her total self now. He admitted to George that she never was popular at school due to her solid and wholesome views toward loose morals. When she came home from the first meeting with George, Ted could see a new look in her eyes. Fran had fallen completely and hard into this love thing. Even as a child, she had never shown as much excitement for any presents or gifts, like most young kids did. So Ted had known and when he began to dig into her new personality, he found a pure deeply seated love in her. She had never been around these feeling before and this made her somewhat unpopular at school even though she was a beautiful girl. Once Ted had found out about George, he did some checking around the post and found him to be a very strong and upstanding soldier. Ted had seen himself 20 years ago in George. George thanked him for all his direction and trust. Fran was not going into this life with George wearing blinders. She knew very well what might happen. Ted had told her to live for today and hopefully the tomorrows would help themselves. Ted was finally sold on George when Fran had came home after the guys had told the girls what lay ahead in their lives. This attempt by George and the others to let the girls off easy was a strong point for them. Most

CHAPTER SIX

guys would have taken what they could get and leave before they were hooked. Ted and the other fathers involved had talked things through many times. The main force they kept hitting was a vision of their new daughters and how much they were showing a deep strong love. When everything else fails, love would be the one item to carry on helping everyone.

The girls finally came in from the kitchen and sat down with the men. Now there was only family talk going. George told the family that he wasn't sure about being out here during the weeknights and he would get with the First Sergeant tomorrow to see. In the morning, he and the other soldiers would have to leave about 5:30 to make sure they got to the company formation on time. They could eat breakfast in there. George did have uniforms here and he would wear the fatigues in and if the uniform changed, he could change in the barracks again. The family talked for about an hour more and then George figured he needed to get some rest for the morning. Everyone said good night and the couple walked down to their basement room. Morning came fast and George rolled out of bed at 4:30. He got ready for work and kissed Fran goodbye. He would call if he couldn't get back tonight. George drove around to the other guys' places and picked them up for the ride back to the post. They arrived at the post by 6 and reported in. George asked the

A CROWN OF GLORY

First Sergeant about living off post with his wife. The First Sergeant saw nothing wrong with this as long as they could get to work each morning. They all had phones available there also, so the company could get a hold of them if needed. So the approvals were made. The First Sergeant asked George if he wanted to apply for home ration credit. George told him no as he could eat breakfast and lunch here. That sounded like a good plan. The guys next went to breakfast and stood formation for assignments. The old workweek was starting again.

George told Bill and Bob he would wait here for them when he got off, or they could wait for him. The plan was made. Each soldier went to their assigned tasks for the day. The day ran onward and finally it came quitting time. George thought the day had passed at a snails pace. Finally the three met at the barracks and each grabbed a clean uniform for the morning. They needed to take their laundry bags to their new homes now. They could bring their laundry in once a week and turn it in to the laundry on post. This would save work for the wives. They had enough just getting through school now. As time continued, the men probably would bring most of their uniforms home and leave only one each of dress and fatigue in case of something coming up. They would also maintain their footlockers in inspection

CHAPTER SIX

shape. The three drove off post to head home. Seemed a little funny to be doing this now. Especially since none of the three had ever had any intention of getting married just a month ago. George came into the town and he needed gas so he drove into the gas station here. The man filled it up and checked the oil. Everything was fine. Bill and Bob dug out some money to pay for the gas. They said they were riding and since George was using his car, they could at least furnish the gas.

Everyone got home and George ran into the house to grab his wife and give her a big smooch. He told her it was all right with the company if he stayed here as long as he could get to work and had a phone available if they needed him other times. So for now this was settled. He told her that the others had volunteered to pay for the gas for the ride to post everyday. He told Fran about the separate rations thing, and now he had thought to go ahead with this. He could still eat in the mess by paying the amount and yet would get some money for evening and weekends. He had figured this out during the day. Tomorrow he would inform the First Sergeant. George was thinking they could give this money to her parents. It might help some. George told Fran about his thoughts on the laundry also. He would leave one set of each uniform in the barracks and the rest would be here. He would still use the post laundry so she wouldn't have to worry about minor things. George asked Fran where her parents were. She told him they had drove into the post to get some groceries. George went downstairs to change clothes and Fran caught him off guard. She came at him with a grizzly bear look. The attack was on. And he didn't have to worry about taking his uniform off at all. Boy, she was something else. He had one hell of a girl here, and they both knew it. 30 minutes later, George weakly pulled a change of clothes on. Fran just sat on the bed smiling at him. He asked if she had learned this in school but she told him this was OJT action.

The two lay on the bed and talked. This was a very peaceful relaxing time and they always liked talking to each other. George asked Fran if she could drive a car. He had never even thought about things like this. She told him she could since her father had trained her very well. This was good if he would get transferred. They lay there talking, some about important things and others about nonsense things. A good blend of conversation was carried on.

CHAPTER SEVEN

Fran's parents came home a few minutes later and George went upstairs to see if he could help with anything. Fran's mother must have bought out the commissary with all this. George now told Ted that he would apply for separate rations in the morning and this might help them a little. Ted told him they didn't need the money, but George was going to get it for them anyway. George told Ted that his First Sergeant had agreed for him to live out here. He also advised what his plan was for his uniforms. Ted seemed to think everything was acceptable now. Ted was wondering if Bill or Bob might get a car themselves soon. He didn't want to depend upon his totally incase something went wrong with it, they could still get to work. Ted told George that he could always use their car but George told him this would hinder everyone from the normal routine. In an emergency they might have to get Ted to drive them in however.

Ted asked Fran how school was today. She told them it was a riot. Seems every kid knew by now and even the teachers had found out. This all was front line news. Fran had been embarrassed by some remarks that some kids had made, but she knew these were the type to never get anywhere themselves. Many of the girls had come to Fran and the other girls and questioned them about their old reputation and now falling so fast and so far. They had agreed that when you found the right man, you needed to grab fast. The teachers had even complimented them on their new shining faces. They could see the improvement through their love. So overall things had gone basically as they expected them to. Fran had heard from some of her girl friends that guys had been wondering what these service men had to get these 'icy' girls turned over so fast. There wasn't much talk about them having to get married since everyone knew there would no way a person could find out if they were pregnant in this short of time. To many of the girls, this was a lesson in life as to get what you wanted and leave no avenue for escape.

CHAPTER SEVEN

The normal routine continued and things were going fairly well. The company on post had started holding one day a week for reviewing infantry tactics. This generally was scheduled for Wednesday. There were many infantry companies here on the post and they began training throughout the week. This increase of training was a small warning that things were not looking good over in Korea. George had been married now for a month and a half and was doing well at home and at the post. George and Ted had been watching the Korea problem grow. On a Tuesday morning formation, the CO came out to address the soldiers. He told the company that he had received the word early this morning. This company with five others on the post was on a 30 day alert for transfer to Korea. He told the soldiers this was not the final word as they could be cancelled at any time. The fact was that more than likely this would go through. He asked that all married soldiers see him in his office sometime today. Bob, Bill, and George walked to the orderly room as soon as formation was over. The CO greeted them and asked them in. His records of them had indicated none had taken any leave since joining the Army. He now recommended that these three apply for at least a three week leave. They would need the last week here to help in getting things ready for shipment with the company. He also advised them to go to the Judge Advocate on post and make sure their insurance was made up correct if they wanted to name their new wives as benefactors. Generally they should think about a power of attorney form for them also, in case they needed to do something here for the men over there. If the soldiers were OK with this, he would give them the day off on VOCO and start their leaves tomorrow. The three men thanked him and George told him he was sure this company would do well with a good commander like him. The CO also told them to bring all their uniforms and equipment with them in the last week. They would be issued field gear once they arrived in Korea. The three men saluted the CO and left. They headed out toward home with their bad news.

When George came home, Ted knew something was up. George proved him right as he told Ted. The bad part would be with Fran after she came home from school. George and Ted talked and they mentally drew a list of things the couple needed to do now. Basically things were simple since only personal problems would need to be fixed if possible. This included the insurance and such. George was glad he had Ted here to help him. When Fran came home she was shocked to see George here. She asked him why he was home so early, then instantly came to the conclusion. George told her he had three weeks leave and then a week

CHAPTER SEVEN

later it looked as if they would be sailing. Fran looked funny and ran to the bathroom. George was concerned, but Ted told him this was a normal reaction for many girls. George waited until she came out and he grabbed her and held her tight. She was still crying some, but slowly was getting things under control. She was still holding George tight and not saying anything. Finally she straightened up again and looked George in the eye. Her look told him everything. She could not stand to loose him. She had just started into her adult life with a lover so fantastic he could not be replaced. There was not much talking available right now. She would have to accept the unchangeable facts and attempt to gain from what was left.

The four family members now sat in the living room for a while. Slowly Fran started to talk again. She was sorry the way she had acted. George and Ted both told her there was no problem. This news was rough on everyone, including her parents. Everyone knew this had a good chance of coming, and everyone was hoping it wouldn't. Ted was saying that his wife had acted very much the same when he got the transfer during WWII. He was hoping that George's tour would not be as long as his was. He had spent three years in the Europe areas before getting any idea of returning to normal again. Ted did not think this would last very long due to the countries involved. Fran sat with George and was pressing very tight against him. He really loved this girl and did not want to leave either. Army regulations did not specify any difference between married and non-married soldiers. George could imagine the other two soldiers going through the same thing right now. Thank God the fathers all were ex-infantry soldiers from a real war. Ted now recommended that they all drive to the post and he would treat them to dinner at the club there. In his mind he was thinking that Fran needed to see other men who had received alerts this day also. She might see how many men took the alert for transfer. It had helped with her mother, so now it was her turn. Fran kept apologizing for her upset, but her mother told her this was a normal first reaction. She did not remember when her dad got his orders but mother had acted just like she was. All this was showing was the love she held for George. Her mother told her to never apologize for this.

The four arrived at the club and Ted signed everyone in. They were taken to the dining room and seated at a table. George's First Sergeant was here also. He walked up to the table and spoke with Ted. They had known each other for years. The sergeant asked if this was a tone down from today. Ted smiled and told him it was. The both laughed now. All the old salts knew what was happening with the young soldiers. They had gone through this also in their past. The waiter came by and got the order and now different people, many that George didn't know, were coming up and saying hi to Ted. They all told him they had got the word today also. Ted introduced George and told them he had also, and this was his son-in-law and daughter. Some had heard but many had not yet. A waiter came from the bar and asked if anyone wanted a drink. Ted ordered for everyone at the table. Of course George was not much of a drinker. Ted laughed and told him he would be before long in Korea. George was noticing that Fran was picking up some now. Soon she was laughing along with everyone else. Over two-thirds of the customers here had stopped by to greet the main man and George. They all had their assignments also. It looked as if Leavenworth would be vacated within a month. The foursome ate dinner and drank a couple more drinks. Finally they headed back home. George knew something about Ted's career, but he saw now that the man was a true hero to everyone around. Fran had perked up a long way. George thanked Ted for the evening and for Fran's relief.

When they got home, Fran was very tired, maybe some from the drinks, so she headed downstairs. George went also after thanking Ted again. Everyone had seen the change in Fran and lucky that Ted and his wife knew it also.

A CROWN OF GLORY

George came downstairs and Fran was waiting for him. The both crawled in bed and Fran became glued to George. They lay here hardly talking. They were just holding each other and thinking the same thoughts. Fran apologized again for the way she had acted. George told her he was honored the way she acted. It probably meant she would go looking for another guy a couple of weeks after he was gone. Fran hit him and cursed. George laughed again. Now Fran got busy with her agenda. George just held her and thought wonderful thoughts. If he never came back, this had been worth every moment. Ted had told him this was the way to feel anyway. George and Fran had a love that was almost unmatched at least among people they knew. They had three whole weeks to explore each other yet. Fran was talking about pulling out of school. George would love this, but didn't want her to know. He told her she really needed to graduate. He had an idea for her to check and see if under the circumstances if she could pull out for the three weeks and take out of school assignments. She could be with George and still be in line to graduate if they allowed this. She was holding a very good grade average anyway. This day had been wearing on everyone. Things had moved too fast for normal conceptions, but Fran and George still were meeting things head on. The couple finally got to sleep and had a

CHAPTER SEVEN

good night anyway. The last exercise might have helped get them into sleep. Fran needed to go to school in the morning and find out about the three week absence. As morning came, Fran was the first up and then George got around. He was going to walk her to school today, just for the exercise. They got some breakfast and walked toward the school. Fran was enjoying this walk as she was showing off her love to everyone on the streets. At the school, George gave Fran a kiss and let her walked on to the building. George walked back to the house. He sat and drank coffee now. He read part of the newspaper that Ted had already read. Things were really going downhill in Korea. George was not real sure what he would do for the day until Fran came back home.

He did not have to wonder very long. Fran came dancing in and told everyone she had been excused from school for the next month. She only had to do assignments they gave her here at home. She was very excited since now she could really live like a married woman for a short time. She had gone to the principles office first off. He did not see much problem with her request, but she needed to ask her teachers also. Everyone was willing to help her due to her resolve to finish school and her high grade average. All this thrilled Fran and many friends at school were happy for her to get off. They all had seen a real change in Fran since her marriage. She was probably one of the most enlightened students here now. Her two other friends, Ann and Sandy had learned from Fran and had managed to get the time off also. They all would spend this time with their lovers.

CHAPTER EIGHT

Time now was sailing by with not much delay for anything. The soldiers were spending every minute they could with their wives. There probably was more love being expended in this town than around the world generally. Of course this was the parents' thought. They loved seeing their daughters so happy and in love. As this week passed, they found there was another grange dance on Saturday. They all wanted to go, as these were great entertainment plus just having fun with their loves. This dance went as most did and the kids were home by 11. They couldn't believe that a week had already passed. They spent time at the lakes close by and walked around some also. George would of course, leave the car here with Fran. He didn't think she would have any trouble with it, but her dad could probably help if she did have some problems. Everything was slowly shifting over to the girls. They would have complete control of everything when the guys were gone. Many things would be on their shoulders and this would be training for the future also. The girls had all talked with their mothers and found many things they needed to do. The six of them drove out to the base and went to the Judge Advocates place. They had to get things here changed over, such as the insurance and the power of attorney. None of the three guys were concerned about what the girls could do with this much authority. When they got to the car after getting these things finished, George told the other two that the girls now owned them. They probably would cash out and dump them the first week they were gone.

The group went to the company orderly room to see what was happening so far. Things were still in the works for the movement. The CO had asked to see the three if they came in. So they entered his office. He invited the girls in also. He made a small speech and handed the guys a piece of paper. This was orders, promoting them to Corporals. This was a real shock and they were below the average service time for this. The CO told them they would have been promoted as soon as they hit Korea anyway, so he wanted to get this done now. This was a nice increase of pay also. And the girls were allowed to check on post housing if they might want to. The CO excused the couples and wished the girls well. He told them he would take care of these goofy guys for them. Everyone thanked the CO. He was one hell of a commander.

The guys checked with the company clerk if there were any other things they needed. There was nothing at this time anyway. So the couples headed back home. They all were excited about the promotions. There would be some substantial increases in pay now. As George let them out, the couples would run for the house. They had some good news to tell for now. This rank would give them positions as assistant squad leaders also. Whether this was important in combat, no one of them really knew. Now everyone was glad of the new news and wanted to celebrate some how. The three fathers decided it might be time again to head for the club on the post and have a celebration dinner here. So everyone loaded up and they headed for the club. As the last time went, so would this evening. Everyone in the club seemed to know all the retired men with the group. They definitely had a reputation about the base here. George figured that Ted was well known all over from his various decorations. The group had an excellent dinner and drinks after this. They finally headed home about 9 and were talking all at once again. The young soldiers were learning from the older ones and they could see what might lie ahead for them. The night had relieved some more concerns now and the young couples were ready to battle another week.

When George and Fran got home, they thanked her parents for the night and headed to the basement. The drinks had started things and they wanted to get involved now. The young couple attacked each other and the night drew on. They finally fell into sleep and dreamed good dreams for the future. This second week was running fast also. At least Fran was home with George all day. They spent a lot of time in the back yard, sitting and talking. George was almost getting ready to go now. He had met so many older servicemen who had been where he was going that he figured to get it over and come home. His lovely wife was growing daily toward a future life with George. This would be the way to think now. He would be only going to another assignment. George could think of nothing more to get ready so his time was totally with his lovely wife and her family. Ted was helping a lot in soothing concerns Fran had. The name of the game seemed to be go and not think any bad thoughts. Fran was required to finish certain assignments for her classes and turn them in to the school each week. She had

CHAPTER EIGHT

been doing well with this and George was very proud of her. He really wanted her to finish high school, even though many people did not in this day and age.

In the third week, Ted gave George a small camera to carry in Korea. Ted had carried it all over Europe and now he thought George should have a go at it. He told George if he couldn't get it developed over there just send the roll back here with paper wrapped around it to protect the film. Ted was funny in the fact that he came up with something everyday for George to remember or think about. He had many stories and incidents that he told George about. Each item was going to be helpful to George over there. George and Fran had spent almost every hour together over the three weeks. They had grown far forward toward their already massive love they held for each other. This was for George and Fran to remember while they were separated. During the final weekend, the families all got together again at the city part for a last picnic. The day was fantastic for everyone and a very enjoyable time out. In the morning, the three soldiers had to return to the post and begin getting ready for the final leg of the journey. The three young soldiers had obtained professional wallet photos of their loves. And the girls had some larger ones of the guys. The afternoon ended toward evening again and everyone headed for home. George told the others he would get them about the same time as before. Fran and George had already figured on her driving the three for the last day here. She could then bring the car back home.

The morning came way too fast and the guys were not glad to be getting up again so early. They did their morning routines and George kissed Fran and drove off. He picked the other two up and they drove to the post. George parked in the company parking lot and they walked to the mess hall for breakfast. After this they attended formation. Assignments were made and they all had to do with loading company property on a train that was sitting on a siding not far from the company area. The days ahead were involved with moving almost everything the company had. This train would transport the equipment to San Diego for loading aboard a ship there. This train would be sent off ahead by one day of the troops. They would ride a train there also. Time ran very fast through this week and finally the day came when everyone would leave. George had to pull himself away from Fran as did the other two guys. They said their good byes and Ted drove them to the base. He thought this might be easier on Fran. So they three arrived at the company street and reported in. George said his goodbye to

CHAPTER EIGHT

Ted and Ted left, leaving his known world to the basic army once again.

The soldiers were all sent to the mess hall for breakfast and a sack lunch for the train. About two hours later, the train, loaded with men from Leavenworth pulled out. They were on the road now. It was a very slow trip. The train would stop every so far and load sack lunches for the men. It took into the next day before the train arrived at San Diego. Here they unloaded on the waterfront. There was a huge ship sitting here painted gray. This was their next transportation. The day after their arrival here, they were aboard the ship. It was not a pleasant place. The smell of body order, oil and other things was predominating on board. Fortunately by afternoon the thing began to move. The trip was scheduled to take three weeks and this was really a nice thing for everyone to hear. There already were sick troops on board. The three soldiers had no idea how they might do, but there was no choice now. The second week was beginning to wear on everyone. Half the soldiers were sick and the other half probably would be soon. Food was not an option any more. You ate what you might keep down and gave the rest to the sharks. The stench in the sleeping area was enough to get to anyone. George and the other two soldiers managed to stay on deck most of the time.

A CROWN OF GLORY

The third week came and left. The PA system on board advised everyone that the ship now was approaching Korea. The soldiers would be unloaded and the freight after that. The debarking from the ship went well as all the soldiers wanted to get on solid ground again. Company areas had been set up and the members had to find their place. As the companies were reformed, then they were marched over to a large building and were issued field gear. The next step was issuing weapons to everyone. The companies were sent to other areas to pitch tents and a headquarter area. The men were told they would be here until they figured how to send them to other places. The soldiers were given no ammo as yet. This would be issued as they began to move out. Things were sounding more and more like a forced march type of transfer for the men. This was the first chance for the guys to write a note home. They had been given an address for people at home to write to them. As things began to organize once again, the rumor mill was running full blast. Nothing about this information was probably true, but gave people something to do. Finally, the company was formed and the CO addressed the men. This company was to be transported partially by truck up north. The trucks arrived and the company was loaded on them. They had their basic equipment including mortars and machine guns. Ammo was issued now also, but everyone was warned not to load any until they were off the trucks. George, remembering what Ted had told him, loaded his clips for easy loading in the rifle if needed. The trucks headed out and the road was rough. The Koreans evidently did not have much for road working equipment. The two and a half ton trucks were rough riding anyway. The men rode along for over three hours and were wondering if they were headed to China. Finally the trucks pulled into a clearing and the men were told to off load here.

The troops were issued some rations to carry with them and given a hot meal here. From here they would be walking according to the rumor mill. After the meal, the men were checked for cleaning their mess kits and formed into a platoon sized group. This way the company began to walk forward. They could hear cannon fire way ahead and they had no idea where they were. After a couple of hours, the CO was on the radio and talking to someone. The company was ahead of the place they were supposed to be The CO was ordered to set here and wait for flank units to come up. The CO gave the order for everyone to load and lock their weapons. The CO ordered the company to seek cover and if none was available to dig for it. This CO was a damned good combat man. The troops had just found enough cover when a whistle was heard. The CO yelled for everyone to watch forward. This order was transmitted down the line of troops.

The fear factor increased with immediate speed. A charge of enemy soldiers was seen heading toward the company. The commander told everyone to fire at will; make sure you had a target. The enemy seemed to have a large number of troops but the withering fire from the company ate them down rapidly. The company mortars were firing now also. Machine guns had been set up and they were firing also. After about 15 minutes the firing ceased. Platoon sergeants were yelling for casualty reports. The company had suffered three wounded and none killed. Corpsmen were called and first aid given until they could get the men back to doctors in the rear. This had been a small engagement for the company and the CO called his praises for his men. Welcome to Korea someone yelled.

CHAPTER NINE

The CO was on the radio again and was getting orders. The company was to hold here and wait as before. The CO passed orders on to dig in and hold for now. The men were learning very fast. When they were told to dig in and wait, this they did. The CO walked the line and praised his men for their first combat experience. They had done very well. The company relaxed for now and guys began to walk around. The CO passed orders that everyone stay behind cover as snipers could be out there. About this time a shot was fired and a private dropped dead. Bad deal. Everyone now understood that this was a killing zone. Shortly a whistle was heard again and the enemy began running forward once again. This time, they looked like they were twice the size of the last bunch. Everything began firing again. This fire-fight lasted almost 30 minutes. The casualty count this time was five wounded, two dead, counting the first private. Everyone was now getting the picture that this was no holiday.

The CO called in and asked for some fire support. There was nothing close enough to them he was told. He asked for medical evacuation and got the same answer. He now got mad and asked if any bastard back there knew where the company was. His orders remained to hold his position. He told them his position was about to be overran unless he got some support. The battalion commander, a major, finally came on line and told the CO was move back two miles. Here was a couple other companies anyway. So the CO ordered a withdrawal back. The men liked how the CO handled this. The company pulled back and the CO went to see the battalion commander. He had lost two men killed and some wounded because of some stupid bastard that had no idea where they were. The Major agreed and told the CO that he had handled this incident by removing some ranks from the command. A man lost by necessary combat was normal, but to kill men with stupidity was much worse.

The company was ordered to dig in here and hold for now. This they all did from the last experience. Night was coming fast and the positions were laid out to effect a good

CHAPTER NINE

field of fire.   Night could get very dark and with no help to see, the men had to listen hard.   The mortars with the company had some flares to be used if necessary.   The CO did not want to waste them however.   He ordered the line to hold and not call for flares unless they were sure they heard enemy crawling up to their line.   This first week in Korea was a total new learning experience to the company.   Even old soldiers who had came through WWII had to think hard about what the enemy might do next.   This enemy was not like those in the last war.   Everyone was learning more and more.   The action now was a new game and everyone was having to review past experience and new tactics.   Now sergeants were walking the line and talking low to new troops.   They were at a loss also, and the new men needed to understand that they were doing very well under these circumstances.   The company had lost two men this day and the future might hold a lot more.   This brief encounter today was looking at the future of the combat here.   These enemy men were committed to their goal of taking the south part of this nation.

George was amazed that the company was still here at all.   Of course he had never seen such combat and was trying to learn as he went.   He knew now that a person needed cover to protect them.   The CO told the troops to pair off and have one alert while the other got some rest.   This way the troops might get some rest. This had been a strongly learned day so far. The CO came around again slowly giving cheer to the troops and thanking them for this fighting day. He was telling everyone that he was proud of his company. The thought process for the mind changes very broadly from the first combat moment and hopefully led the man forward. This night drug by quietly and no enemy was heard or seen. The morning came brightly. The days were getting chilly now in the evenings and mornings. The company was holding for any new orders but none were coming down. At times fire could be heard in different directions. Some one was getting hit on the line was the guess. The company held where they were and waited orders. The day was getting boring but nothing came over the radio to the CO. He must have scared someone about the company's last combat incident. George was getting the idea that in Korea, there was a bunch of idiots playing chess. No one but the company CO seemed to know what to do. As before, George had made a commitment to follow this commander to the end of the combat, if this was required. The CO had played everything correct that George had seen. George wanted to get home alive, so he would follow the commander here.

Night came in again and the company still held their same positions. It was darker than last night George thought.

CHAPTER NINE

About 2 in the morning, a guard thought he heard noises. He passed the word down the line and the mortars fired a flare. All of a sudden there were over 50 enemy as close as 15 yards. The light helped and the company men extinguished most of them on the first firing burst. The firing stopped as the light went out, the CO called for another mortar flare. This was just to see if there were any other enemy close here. The last attack must have ended their bravery, as there was nothing else coming as far as it looked. The company stood their ground and waited for a new attack. Nothing came. The morning came and the company had no new instructions. The radio finally cranked up and told the company to move forward about 500 meters. The CO ordered the front movement. This was daylight and the enemy had not been sighted as yet. In their new position the men dug in once again. They were ready to sit here now. The enemy had different ideas about this. The company had not been in their new position for 30 minutes when everyone heard the whistle blow. The company immediately got ready and met the oncoming enemy head on. The whole company had learned to expect almost instant trouble. The enemy came running forward and shooting as they came. The firefight did not last long as the company dropped more than they were. This time they suffered only one dead and 3 wounded.

A CROWN OF GLORY

This was a good figure according to the battalion commander. The men had fought very well. The company had gained notice by the upper commanders and this was not good with the men. They were fighting for their CO, not higher jerks. A major walked the company line. He made the mistake of asking George what he was fighting for. George told him straight out. He was fighting for his commanding officer. The major asked George if he was happy to be here, and then George told him like it was. He was an American and forced to fight for another country that was generally too stupid and afraid to fight for them selves. George didn't really care if the major got upset or not. He didn't say anything more, just turned and walked away.

A sniper began again and anyone who was up and moving around was in danger. George looked very hard and could not see him anywhere. Bill had jumped into the hole with George. Bill made a small noise and pulled his rifle up to his shoulder and fired. Way ahead, George saw a man fall from a tree. Bill had seen the sniper and shot him. The company now just sat and waited for what ever might happen next. A couple of guys came around passing out ammo. George opened a small can of something from his pack. You had to eat as you found the time. The CO had finally found someone behind that could get things moving. The artillery

CHAPTER NINE

was ready and began firing just forward of the company. They let loose a huge mass of incoming shells and seemed to wipe the ground of everything. It sure opened a clear field of fire out there. George appreciated this, as did everyone in the company. There shouldn't be any problem for a while now. The enemy was probably mowed down like the trees. Of course you could never understand the idiots in the rear. You cleared one area in front and they would move you up past this and into a dangerous area again. The company saddled up once again and moved about 1000 meters forward. They stopped just as they began receiving fire from the front. The enemy evidently did not like them in this spot, as they came again on a dead run. The time, the battle was on and raged for about two hours. The company took a heavy toll this time. They lost 30 men wounded, and 10 killed. The wounded were bad and they had no way of getting them back to aid. The medic with the company had run out of most things he carried. There was no re-supply available. This was quickly turning in a huge mess. George would like to see that major up here now. Of course these types of men hid behind when any action started. It wasn't very long before most of the company was talking about the chicken commanders in the rear. The CO here was the only officer in the whole area that knew what he was doing. The company needed a truck or jeep to begin carrying the wounded back. The CO was talking on the radio with someone and could get nowhere regarding transportation. The CO finally went off. He called the colonel he was talking with a stupid bastard and told him if they didn't get some transportation up here, he would pull the company off and they would carry his wounded back. The colonel had told the CO that equipment in the rear was there so they didn't get hit. The old man wanted to get a shot at the colonel!

There was a lot of dumb ass officers back there. Most had never been out of the states, let alone in combat. Finally a couple of trucks came forward and the company men began loading the wounded on them. The dead could wait until later. The two trucks had just left the area when everything started all over. A heavy force was coming full out toward the company. From what everyone was saying on the radio, this company was the only one getting hit. The CO asked for replacements but he was told there were none available. He told someone on the radio that if they sent some of the stupid officers back there up, they might learn what combat was really like and how to use their men better. The CO was not making brownie points with the rear, but he was feeling better anyway. This fight lasted on and off for over three hours. The company was burning up ammo rapidly. The CO called for ammo, rear told him that had no way to get up to him. He told them he was pulling back then. A colonel came back on the radio and ordered him to stay where he was. The CO had words with him and told the colonel to get his stupid ass up here and fight without ammo. A jeep was sent forward with ammo.

Everything the company received they had to fight for tooth and nail. If the company had anyone else for a CO, they probably would have been wiped out by now. Everyone here was beginning to wonder what kind to idiots were in charge back there. By this time, the company had lost almost half its manpower either as wounded or killed. George, Bill and Bob were still going however. A couple of times, George had thought he might have to fix his bayonet and fight it out hand to hand. This was a very nasty area and it was looking like the enemy wanted this spot for some reason. The CO was on the radio again requesting replacements. He gave his casualty rate and since no other unit was under siege like this, he needed replacements to hold on. The battalion finally advised he would be getting what they could scrape up.

A CROWN OF GLORY

CHAPTER TEN

A s the evening drew closer, the battle was easing off. This gave everyone a chance to get more ammo and something to eat if they wanted such. George and Bill were still doing well on the line. Platoon leaders came around asking how their men were doing. It seemed amazing that the company had anyone left. This had been a very hard day of combat that most people could have never guessed. The platoon leaders were telling the men to keep one man awake in each foxhole. The others needed to rest as they could. They also needed to switch on and off with this. Nights were not void of action as the company had already found out. Around 3 in the morning, men began hearing low noises. Finally the mortar fired a flare and it shown on the enemy edging forward. This time the company opened up with what they had, including the machine guns. The mortar crew basically managed to keep a flare up most of the time. They were beginning to run short on these however. George ran short of ammo and yelled for replacement. His lieutenant came crawling up with more ammo. George thanked him and continued firing forward. George had felt a sting to his arm and figured some bug had nailed him. This fight began losing ground before an hour was up. Everyone was awake now and finally the sun arrived. The ground in front of the company was totally littered with dead enemy. The company troops began re-supplying their ammo. George and Bill were scooping out the area in front of their foxhole. Bill turned to George to say something and he got a shocked look on his face. George looked at him and Bill pointed to George's arm. There was blood over his whole sleeve. That was the bug sting he thought. A round had hit his arm and only a flesh wound so no bad damage was done. The medic came by and checked the arm our, then bandaged it better. The medic made a note in his book that he carried. Bill made a joke about George faking a wound just so he could get a Purple Heart. Thisreally made them both think however. If you could get

CHAPTER TEN

wounded in the arm, you could just as well be hit in the head. A few inches difference could mean life or death.

The day was calm now and the troops were tired. The CO told everyone to rest except for one man per hole. George told Bill to get some rest, he would watch at first. A jeep came up from the rear and delivered more ammo, C-rations, and some mail. The mail was a surprise. George got a letter from Fran. She was writing as though she could still see him. Everything at home was doing fine. She had been listening to the radio every evening to hear what was going on over there. Of course she knew that the news would not cover George, but she could almost see him as the radio news went on. George read and reread the letter over and over. Just to have Fran's letter was a big thing now. Bill didn't get one yet so he would have to wait. George did tell of any news about town. Bill now told George he would watch for a while so George could get some rest. This was about all a person could do for now. Those damn night raids were horrible and they sure took a man's rest away. Noon had just passed when some rifle fire began. Everyone was up and now a machine gun started to talk. This gun was dangerous as it was firing very short bursts, which generally meant a person was targeted with each burst. Bill was watching and finally found where the gun was located. He pointed it out to George. The

A CROWN OF GLORY

CO sent word around to see if anyone had spotted the gun. Bill sent word back and then he crawled out of the foxhole and see about sneaking up on the position. George couldn't let him go alone, so he came after him. They couldn't cover much ground at a time, but this was safer than trying to run at the gun. The men in the company watched as the two creped slowly forward. They wasted almost 30 minutes before they were very close to the gun. As the gun began firing to their left, Bill jumped up and charged the position with his M-1 firing. George came behind and was firing also. Bill ran out of ammo in his gun and threw a hand grenade. This took care of the gun and the men in the position. Now they had to get back to their line. They were on a headlong run back. Some more enemy opened up. The company fired cover rounds for the two. About 20 feet short of the line, Bill was hit hard. As he dropped, he called to George. George grabbed Bill and pulled him into the foxhole. He yelled for the medic. Bill had been hit in the chest. The medic came over and treated him but he needed more help than the medic would give him. He had to be evacuated back to the rear for a surgeon. The CO got on the radio and called back for a jeep. This time, one was sent right up. George and the medic lifted Bill into the jeep and it took off. George was really worried now since Bill looked very bad. The medic told

CHAPTER TEN

George he probably wouldn't make it. This was a hard blow for George. Bob came over now and he had seen everything. The CO made a note and he would get a Silver Star for his attack of the gun position. George asked if the CO would keep him and Bob advised about how Bill was doing. The CO knew these three were very close and he told them he would keep tabs on Bill for them.

The other side had become quiet now. They didn't have their machine gun to help cover them. George was sure there would be one coming up soon. George felt almost hollow inside now. He was worried about Bill. This would really mess things up for the town and Sandy. The girls left would worry way too much if he didn't make it. While George was thinking about this, another attack arose. There looked to be well over a hundred men running forward now. Everyone was instantly busy again. These guys just wouldn't give up. George had used almost a bandoleer of ammo by now. He just kept firing and reloading. Then everything went black. When he saw light again, it was getting dark. The medic checked him out again and told him he had taken a grazing round to his head. He had bled badly as most head wounds do, but otherwise he was going to be just fine. The medic had put a bandage around his head, and it hurt some to put the helmet on. Two hits in less than 24 hours. This was getting serious. The CO received a radio message from the rear. A new company was coming forward and they would replace this company and fall back to the rear for a break. This was fantastic news for all the men. There was a lot of hollering and shouting now. The new company arrived within the hour and the old company fell back. George was hoping he could hear something about Bill. The company arrived at the rear and collapsed on the ground. They all got some chow and clean uniforms. This was real good since George had blood all over his. The small company now began to shape up once again. Living on the line with hardly any rest was very hard on the men. Their company had suffered over 50% losses to wounded or dead. They were to get replacements also while back here. George and Bob began checking on Bill. The medical staff told them he was not here. He had been evacuated to Japan for immediate help there. This group had worked on him and helped his wounds some. He was still alive when he left here. This was at least some news. All Bob and George could do now was hope and pray. Now both men obtained paper and pencils to write a letter back home. They didn't want to say anything about Bill since the military may not have told Sandy anything yet. They kept the letter brief and without much news about themselves. George didn't want to say anything about his minor wounds, as Fran would probably go buggy. Bob did the same with his letter.

It felt wonderful to lie on the ground and not worry about a sudden attack. Everyone got needed rest now. If they could be pulled off line frequently it sure would make things better all around. Everyone was hoping they would be sent to a different area. The one they had been in was one of the worst on the line. The men all ate good now since many times the food did not get to the line very often. You could carry some rations with you, but overall, ammo was more important than food. Many of the remaining men from the start of the company were just mentally out of whack. They would just sit and look at the ground. Everyone had lost friends and you never knew when your turn was coming. George was not alone with more than one wound. As long as a man could still fight, he was kept on line. George was supporting a very strong headache. He walked over to the medical tent and asked for some aspirin. They gave him some and next looked at his wounds. They changed the bandages on both and seemed to think the wounds were doing fine. They asked if both wounds happened at the same time. No but they were within a 24 hour period. The nurse made a note in her book. She told him battalion would have the records and he would be awarded two Purple Hearts. The company stayed in the rear for three days and the guys were almost getting bored. The information finally came to Saddle Up. They were heading out now. They were driven to a new spot on the line. Here they had to dig new foxholes since no one had been here before. They had been assigned this place, as the rear command believed this would be the next hard drive and this company was considered 'seasoned' now.

The men all worked hard to get holes dug. This was a very good way to get protection from the enemy. Every man had a particular method of setting up his foxhole. George had found that a small shelf just below the ground level was needed for storing grenades. Most men also dug a narrow hole toward the back of the foxhole to be used if a grenade came into your hole, you could kick it in the hole and save against a very bad wound. A long time company man John, was assigned to the same hole as George. He had known Bill also and was worried about him. Generally, you did not get very close to replacements since you had enough trouble over friends you made back in the states. War does funny things to men. In a stateside military unit, everyone tries to be friends and then the same unit goes to war, everyone tries to forget friends. Over this short time in combat, many friendships had been totally pulled apart. It just hurts too much when you see a very good friend blown apart next to you.

The men had most of their holes finished and everyone was looking out front, waiting to see or hear the enemy. The company did not have to wait very long. The enemy soldiers came marching forward, four abreast. As they came into range, the company opened up on them. The men just continued to march forward even though they had to step over fallen men. A short time later, the column began breaking off to the sides. There must have been hundreds of them. The company machine gun was running and the mortar was firing also. It seemed like nothing would stop the oncoming troops. George was looking at them and he figured the company had dropped about 200 thus far. There were still that many coming on. The column finally stopped as if by a preannounced plan. The men that were left now sought cover from the company fire. So far the company had held together very well. The new men were getting their teeth set by combat. George did not know of any wounded or killed as yet. The CO was calling around for casualties and was getting no negative information. The enemy below would be set in for now and they would prove a hard group to weed out. A machine gun had been set up down with the enemy and it started it's short burst talking. Everyone knew what this meant. The CO called for volunteers and he got a five men to see if they could take the gun out. The mortar crew put a few rounds very close, but the gun kept its deadly chattering. George was watching the action down around the gun. He conceived a plan about attacking the gun. He came out of his hole and began crawling down the slope. After about 15 minutes, he was about 30 yards from the gun. He was holding a grenade now as he crept closer. No enemy had seen him as yet. He was about 12 yards from the nest and he rose up throwing the grenade. It took the gun and crew out. George was in a rapid withdrawal now and the CO order everyone to fire over him with hopes of keeping heads down as he came back. The other group of 5 were doing the same thing. George had a moment to remember that Bill had been badly hurt doing this. George was about 10 yards from his hole when a bullet came searching for him. It found his shoulder and stung like a mad hornet. He yelled and suddenly two men were pulling him to safety. The medic was on the job instantly. He couldn't tell if anything besides flesh was hurt. At any rate, this man had to be taken back to the rear. The CO radioed for a jeep carrier and it was on its way. The medic told George that he was getting too popular with the enemy. They must be on a first name base as many times that he had been hit.

CHAPTER ELEVEN

The jeep arrived and George was carried to it. He was taken back to the rear and the CO was glad his wound was not real bad. The jeep reached the rear area and George was carried into the medical tent. A doctor was at work on him almost from the flap of the tent. The wound was cleaned and the doctor checked all he could for now. It looked as if the bullet had missed most of the vital areas. George had bled a lot so there must be a torn artery involved. The doctor decided to open part of the area around the bullets entrance. As soon as he did, he found the torn artery and repaired it. The doctor was glad he went into the area. If he hadn't, the wound might have proved fatal by bleeding the man out. He gave George a shot of morphine and bandaged the wound up. Next he checked George's other wounds and replaced the bandages. He shook his head. This man was doing real well in stopping bullets up there. The doctor ordered George to be taken on back to let the latest wound heal some before he was placed on line again. George asked if they could radio up to his company and let them know he was ok. They agreed and the call went out.

George was transported by ambulance bus to the far rear. He was in and out of an alert mode due to the drugs he was getting. He was awake enough to think this trip would be very hard if you didn't have some sort of painkiller. When the bus finally arrived at a hospital, George was carried into the triage area and checked all over. Next he was put in a bed in a very large room. The room was full of other beds and wounded men. George finally fell asleep and must have slept a long time. He was hungry when he woke up. He asked the nurse when chow was. She smiled and told him she would have something up for him right away. She left and came right back. She asked George about the other wounds he had. He told her he had been hired to catch bullets from the enemy and therefore make them run out of ammo. He told her the first two were about 24 hours apart and this last one was about 6 days later. She laughed and told George he should look into changing jobs. This one wasn't so healthy.

CHAPTER ELEVEN

George was told not to sit up and move very much for a while. The doctors here did not want the artery to break open again. So he lay in bed for a week. By then, he was ready to climb the walls. The doctor finally allowed him the sit up for a while tomorrow if everything was still ok. He could walk around some. While he was out before, someone had pined three Purple Hearts to his pillow. He asked about this, and the nurse told him a general had came through and made the awards. George needed to check and see if he could find a small box to send them home. George began walking around now and was able to help some of the guys much worse than he was. The common line of conversations were about where you got hit and during which section of the line. Everyone had heard of George's section. It was known as the worst part of the whole thing. Many of the men had heard that one person here in the ward had been awarded three Purple Hearts. Now they were talking with him. George told them it didn't take much to earn a Purple Heart. The work came in keeping away from them.

George slowly gained in his rebuilding of the body, and he was getting mail here now. This was wonderful just to hear from Fran. He hadn't told her anything as yet. He didn't want to scare her any more than he was now. At home, Ted was beginning to sense something about George.

A CROWN OF GLORY

He was writing way too much and giving very little information. Ted, having been through this already, had figured that George was hurt. He did not mention this to his wife or Fran. George had been at the rear hospital about two weeks when along came Bob. He had been chewed up some by a grenade. He had lost part of a lung and was somewhat scared up. The two friends sat and talked for hours almost. He hadn't told anyone back home about his wounds either. Ann had asked him if he was wounded. Her dad had figured like Ted did and had mentioned this to Ann. Now Bob did not know what to say. Ann also told him that Sandy had received information from the Army that Bill was alive and in a stateside hospital for now. This was great news to Bob and George. Bob intended to talk with the chaplain next time he came around and see what he thought about telling family back home about wounds.

George was getting much better now and he expected to head back toward the front. Bob was already advised that he would be going home as soon as he could travel. George was teasing Bob that he had more Purple Hearts than Bob had. Bob came back with the fact that he was going home soon and George would probably retire from the Army over here. That would really be scary. The days now began to drag along. George was anxious to get out of here, even if it was toward the front again. Finally a doctor gave George the ok to head back up front. George said goodbye to his buddy and wished him a good trip back home. George caught a ride toward the front. He arrived at the battalion headquarters and asked about his company. There was no more company. By the records at the battalion, there were only about ten men left from the original company. George knew of three of them. George asked about the CO. He was told he had been killed two weeks ago. This hurt George. So now he needed to be assigned new again. The battalion wanted him to stay here for a while. He could run ammo, food, and new troops up to the front. Three wounds were all a guy needed they told him.

So George began his new assignment. This would be fairly boring George thought. The job was important though and George knew what it was like to run out of ammo. He ran this assignment for over a month and now asked if he could get back on line. He was sure they knew he was one of the old salts with a lot of experience now. He might be able to help some of the newly assigned men to keep them alive long enough to help the end. Finally he was called into the commander's room. The Major tried to talk him out of the move. George was not budging so the major finally agreed and called his clerk to send George off. The Major told George that any time he wanted back just let him know.

George thanked the man and felt ten feet high again. George caught a ride up toward the front. He would have to find his company. He got in the general area and walked off. He was asking about his new company and everyone kept telling him it was to the right. They didn't know how far however. George kept searching and finally found them. He reported to the commander and got his assignment. The captain here was real happy to have George. George was now a sergeant and he could be used to help this new company survive this mess. The captain asked George to be a floater for right now. He could move along the line and help the men get into gear for combat. George agreed. The Captain and George sat down around a map and the Captain explained to him what they had for right now. This part of the line was not busy right now, but it could be at any time. George agreed, as the place his old company had been was less than a quarter of mile on. He told the Captain about this. This was where George was wounded last. The Captain said this must have been where George earned his Silver Star. George looked funny at the Captain and told him it must have been someone else. No, the Captain had this information from battalion when George was assigned here. George's medals include the Silver Star, the Bonze Star, 3 Purple Hearts and the CIB. Well this was new information to George.

CHAPTER ELEVEN

The Captain enjoyed talking with George. He had experienced the nasty line longer than almost anyone up here now. The Captain also knew that George's old company had been wiped out. While the two were talking, George heard the whistle blow. He jumped up to yell to the men the enemy was coming. He looked over the area ahead of this company and saw more enemy soldiers that a person could count. George was yelling for everyone to save ammo and hit what you were shooting at. The machine gunner was running solid fire out. George got to him and told him to shoot small bursts and line up rounds to each target. This was the first improvement now. George ran the line back and forth telling troops what to do and look for. He continued telling them to make each round contact who they were shooting at. As the combat continued, George felt that bee sting again in the left leg. He continued and guiding the men toward development of good combat skills. This round lasted about an hour and then it was finished. George was checking on casualties. They had finished very well. One killed and about 15 wounded. He was reporting to the Captain and the man added another to the wounded count. George was wondering what the Captain was doing. The Captain pointed to George's leg. He had been bleeding so his pant leg was getting very red. The Captain called for a medic. The medic came up and checked George's leg. He cleaned the wound and bandaged it. The bullet had gone through and had only torn muscle. The Captain called back on the radio and asked for transportation for wounded. He also asked for a pair of pants for George.

The Major heard this and asked how George was. His wound was a flesh wound in the left leg. The bullet had gone straight through. The major just shook his head. The stupid jerk, he should have stayed here. The Captain was full of praise about George. He had saved many casualties by working the line and giving new men instructions about this battle. The Major told the Captain to write him up and he could have another Bronze Star. George needed a rest now from the loss of blood during the fight. So he sat down with the Captain and they talked about line tactics. Most of the things the books told about were out of date since the Civil War. George told the Captain what the men needed to look for next. At least half the men needed to be watching and others resting as they could. The Captain passed this down the line. The one man killed during this last fight was a Staff Sergeant. According to army regulations, battlefield promotions could be awarded to replace a man. The Captain told George he was now a Staff Sergeant. Evening came around and the Captain ordered half the company remain awake at all times. They could alternate between each other in the two man foxholes. Just before total darkness, George walked the line again, checking on fields of fire and telling the men what to listen for. When he returned, he lay down to rest himself. He dozed off and before long was in a sound sleep. He awoke in the wee hours of the morning to gunfire. This was from the company to the left. George ordered a mortar flare to see if anything was going in front of this company. The flare light the area fairly well. Numerous enemy were crawling all around the front. The company had came around the they were shooting now. The machine gun was talking and George could see the enemy dieing everywhere. As one flare would burn out, another was on the way. The enemy didn't stand much of a chance in the bright light. Finally most of the enemy had been cleared from the front of the line and the company to the left was growing quiet. George told the captain that the enemy probably wouldn't attack anymore this night. George lay down once again and dropped off again.

Early the next morning, a nose count of the men was made checking for wounded or dead. There were no serious wounded and no dead. This was due to the early detection of the enemy. They had poked into the other company hoping that this company would be paying attention to the other one.

A CROWN OF GLORY

They could get close enough for a rapid overrun. This had failed with a few flares. The men settled back now, as there was much better rest during the daytime. Nights were always scary mainly because you couldn't see anything. George walked the line again, telling the men what to look for next. He had managed to stay one step ahead of the enemy and this was saving many lives. The Captain was very glad to have George. Each new attack was a learning tool for the new men. Later, they would be just like George.

CHAPTER TWELVE

The next evening George walked the line and talked to the men along it. They had made it through the last night in very good shape. Most of them at least knew what might happen and what to listen for. The night again started along the lines of the night before. No shooting anywhere and no sounds were heard. A coordinated flare posting was tried. Three companies would alternate firing a flare and everyone could get a shadowy picture of what might be out front. If something were seen, the company would shoot a flare where a lineman thought he saw something. The night passed without an attack. This was the first night that had yielded no attack for a long time. The next morning, George was up on the line and checking everything very carefully. He looked for over an hour and could not find anything that was not looking right. He finally walked back to the Captain and talked with him for a short time. He asked the Captain if he would go over and talk to the Captain of the company to their left. The Captain agreed and George asked him to check on their line and if anyone had seen or now found anything not right. The Captain walked over toward the next company. George sat and thought about things.

When the Captain returned, he told George that their company had not seen or heard anything either. This was true last night and so far today. George walked back up on the line and watched again. He came back and now asked the Captain if he could use two squads of men to go on patrol. This shook the Captain as such hadn't been done around here. George told the Captain that he was thinking the enemy had moved out. George was thinking of going out a kilometer and checking around. If this were dead, then they would go out 2 kilometers. He figured 3 kilometers would be enough for this day. The Captain called back to battalion and requested permission to run this patrol. The Major laughed and asked if the man was mentally ok. The Captain told him it was George. The Major immediately came back that if George wanted to go, it was fine with him. Now

CHAPTER TWELVE

George needed to get two squads of volunteers. He passed this down the line. Within ten minutes, he had his volunteers. George talked with the mortar squad and gave them the general coordinates that he might call fire on. The squad sat up and had a couple rounds ready to fire.

George and his squads headed out. They moved easy out of the clear fire zone. Soon they disappeared from sight of the line. The men now increased their intervals to each other. They hit the 1st point and looked carefully around. There was no movement around here over the last 24 hours. George called back to the company and informed them so far. The patrol headed out to the second point. Here George looked very carefully and covered over 200 meters and no movement could be seen. George called this in and advised they were going to the 3rd point. It was the same as the last point. George looked very careful now and still found nothing. This patrol was finished basically having found nothing. The patrol walked back to the line. George reported to the Captain and told him they had seen nothing and he was sure the enemy had left the area. The Captain brought out his maps. George and the Captain looked around the area. The Captain now looked amazed. He knew of a fake plan to bring forces to the west side of the country and act like an amphibious landing was in the works there.

He would bet some very good money that the enemy facing them had been recalled to backup their men in this area. The Captain called for a jeep from the rear. He and George would ride back to the rear area and tell them what looked like might happen. When they arrived back at the rear, the Captain met with the Major. The Captain showed what they thought might be happening. The Major now was shocked also. George had lead the days patrol and found nothing at all. The Major called back further to the Regiment. He talked with a couple of Colonels back there. These men would carry the information back to Army Headquarters. The last Colonel asked if anyone had any recommendation. George told the Major that the frontline should be moved forward 5 kilometers. From here patrols could scout out again. The stepping should continue until the enemy was met once again. This time however, the UN would be meeting the enemy on their terms. As the men moved forward, they could leave the foxholes in and have a return point in case they needed to retreat. The Major got the immediate ok to start this movement. The Colonel asked the officer's name who had this idea. The Major gave the Captain's name and things were looking up.

The front line now began to move forward. The men were glad of this since it was boring just sitting in one place.

CHAPTER TWELVE

The line ran up five kilometers and dug in again. They would be here at least two days to allow the patrols to work. Now, each company would be sending a patrol out. All the companies asked that George come and instruct their men on what to look for. So this first step might take more time. The plan was running now anyway. George asked the Captain who his most experienced sergeant was. The Captain told him that Master Sergeant Craig was this man. So George looked the man up. They talked for a while. George was testing to see if Craig could control the patrol and read sign. Craig was more than happy to go out. George would go with him this time, incase Craig had any questions. The line sat all day and through the night. Still no activity was seen by the troops. This morning, the patrols were saddled up and moved slowly at first. This time they checked up to five kilometers ahead. Same information as the last patrol showing no movement. All patrols arrived back at the line and reported in with the same information. So the companies only needed the two-day halt here. The night ran much like the last few. This routine now ran on. Before any one thought much, the front line had reached 50 kilometers ahead. This was a substantial gain for the UN. This territory had been taken now and it would not be given back. The enemy was extremely upset when they found their territory had been taken back. This front line needed a lot of support now. Regiment sent two more battalions forward for backup. The line battles had become very hard. Many men now were headed back to the rear with bad wounds. The Army was losing more men than they were gaining. The brass in the rear needed to be planning some new replacement methods.

At the current rate, the brass figured that there was a complete Army on each side facing off. The battles were awesome and the casualties were very heavy. George could see no improvement that was available. The troops for the UN needed to be increased by at least two fold. The battles were fought daily with not much give in either direction. A landing by marines where the fake one was planned now became a reality. They were hoping to box the enemy in some with these troops. Days turned into weeks and weeks into months, with no increase in territory for either side. The US troops were spread very thin now and support and supply was almost non-existent. The front line troops were not getting food or ammo at times. This ran downhill and began fights with hand-to-hand combat for many soldiers. George had been in this mess for almost 10 months now. His leg wound was getting into a pain zone now with winter hard to the men. The available clothing was not winter dress. Most of the troops on the line had frostbite injuries by now. Things

CHAPTER TWELVE

got so bad that many had lost toes and fingers and had to be sent home. The supply units with connection to the front lines were screaming for supplies but nothing seemed to be coming.

Every soldier tried everything to help get away from the cold. Most of the men stayed in their foxholes and draped blankets around themselves. Some of the older guys no longer had blankets and they couldn't get any more. The bitter thing was the rear troops had two blankets at the minimum. They also had stoves in their tents. The casualties began to show that cold weather was taking more than enemy fire was. Some troops tried starting fires, but these drew enemy fire and generally were very hard to keep going enough to heat anything. About the only thing troops were thinking about now was the coming spring. George was having the same problems as everyone else. Around the first part of March, a hard push was made by the enemy to punch through the frontline. George's company actually was over run in spots. The battalion sent some relief up and soon pushed the enemy back. The company lost a lot of men during this battle. Over half the company had been lost to wounded and killed. This brought the count down to one man per foxhole for now. The weather was so bad that many men were almost wishing to be a wounded so they could get warmed up again.

Spring finally came back and it was so nice to get warmed up. Most of the men on the line would carry the winter scars for the rest of their lives. Mail had been arriving very slowly. Now George received a letter from Fran. She told him that both Bob and Bill were home now. They both had been medically retired now. Fran was worried about George. The wives had mentioned that their husbands had told them that George had been wounded numerous times. So the cat was out of the bag. George figured he had better tell Fran some news anyway. The army had decided to start relieving companies one at a time for some rear rest. George wondered why they couldn't do this during the cold winter. George's Company was due to pull back next week. This would really be a relief for many men. Two days before the company was due to pull back; the enemy decided it wanted some target practice. This time they began with mortars. George was outside his foxhole when a round came in close to him. He grabbed a lot of shrapnel in his body. Nothing major, just a pain. The fight was hard but didn't last very long.

The day finally came for George and his company to move back to the rear. They moved very gladly back. Just to

CHAPTER TWELVE

finally be able to get warm again. When they arrived back at battalion they were assigned an area that would be assigned to the company. There was a tent set up and it was warm inside. It was a company headquarters tent, so many guys warmed up at once. The Major came over to the company area and called for George. He wanted to talk with him. The army was allowing long-term men in Korea the chance to take a leave home for a month. George needed to think for a minute about this. No one really knew how long this mess would run, and he might not see Fran for a long time yet. He thought about his injuries and could maybe relieve her mind somewhat about him. Finally he told the Major he would like to go. The Major was happy for George, as he knew from the states that he hadn't been married very long until being sent over here. Here he had taken some very hard abuse. The Major started arraignments and asked George if he had a class A uniform. George had his Khaki uniform, which was close. The Major gave George a smaller suitcase and told him to pack up. He would send George back further the next day. So George would begin his hopscotch across the water to home. It took him four days to reach the US. There the military arranged a final military flight toward his home. He had not told Fran or anyone that he was coming home on leave. When he arrived in Fort Leavenworth, he called home.

A CROWN OF GLORY

He got Fran first off and asked if she had any transportation. Yes she did to answer him. Next he asked if she could pick a strange man up at Leavenworth. She almost came unglued now. She grabbed her parents and drove into Leavenworth. George was at the front gate and when they arrived the car was parked and she was already running to George. She was jumping around, giggling and squealing, making all kinds of noise. George finally got to shake hands with Ted and give Fran's mother a quick hug. Ted was driving so George and Fran climbed in the back. Ted took off, but now came some hard questions. Ted had seen George's award ribbons on his uniform. He asked George if he had been in much combat. George told him it hadn't been too bad really. Ted asked him how a guy could get four Purple Hearts if he hadn't been in very much combat. Next he asked about the Bronze Star, the Silver Star and the Legion of Merit awards. He finally nailed George down. George had to admit to some combat above normal. Ted was no ordinary man, and he could see that George had been through hell. Normally he had never heard of a man getting a leave from a rough combat area. Generally the Army kept everyone on line as long as the war was going.

Fran told George about Bill and Bob. They both were home now and medically retired. And they had let some of

CHAPTER TWELVE

the cat out of the bag about George. Bill had been the worst hit. He had told Fran that George and him had taken the machine gun out and this was what sent him home. Bob next came around and told everyone that he had seen George in a rear hospital before moving back to the states. So Fran was wanting some answers.

A CROWN OF GLORY

CHAPTER THIRTEEN

They arrived home and Fran didn't want to let George out of the car. She was hanging on very tight. She finally got out and held partially to him as he climbed out. She noticed when she squeezed him at times he would jump a little bit. She asked about this and he told her he just wasn't used to this yet. Inside, they all sat in the living room. Ted was dragging information out of George slowly. They finally learned about George's wounds and how he won his medals. Ted told George to ease up as he was getting close to him for awards. They both laughed about this. George told them he also had just been hit with shrapnel from a mortar round and this was why he was a little sore in places. Ted had heard the story about the line advance in Korea a few months ago. The newspapers had not mentioned any names but indicated that a couple of old line troops had found a soft spot with the enemy and managed to advance the line over fifty miles forward. This was a substantial step for any war. Ted told George there were peace talks going on in France right now, but there had been no conclusion reached as yet. So now George asked about the local news. What had been happening while he was gone. Basically everything was still running like always. George's pay had increased a large amount by now with all his promotions. The only way a person rose this fast in rank was during a war and the person had to be almost non replaceable. At any rate, the pay had really jumped up. Fran had put most of it in savings for their future. George told every one how nice it was to sit here in comfort with people he loved. There was no danger from enemy troops and you did not have to watch everything all the time. Ted remembered all this also. He and George had marked a trail that most people never traveled.

Now George wanted to change his clothes and get out of his 'monkey' suit. He wondered if his other clothes would fit. He grabbed some and changed. Fran was downstairs with him and when she saw his body, she was shocked. It seemed everywhere he had scares and holes. He laughed and

CHAPTER THIRTEEN

told her they would have to turn the lights off when getting ready for bed so she couldn't see him. She mentioned that now she had seen so she could think of other things to do. She grabbed George and fell on the bed. Now he was under attack from a different opponent. A few minutes later, George and Fran took a fast shower and dressed to go back up stairs. Now George could use a sandwich or something to eat anyway. Fran made him a sandwich when they came back upstairs. Ted wanted to know if he needed to get more energy now and he smirked. This was almost embarrassing. Later, George wanted to stop by Bob and Bills places to see then for a few minutes. They had been buddies in sharing the war for a while. They were just unlucky to get hit so badly. George asked Fran how the old car was running. She told him it very seldom ran, as she had no place to go unless she wanted to go with her parents.

She told George that she had thought she was pregnant after he left, but it turned out she wasn't. She had almost wished she were. But maybe next time. George asked Fran how she thought about him getting out or staying in the military. She really hadn't thought about it very much. George was past his original draft time but he was extended for now. He could reenlist anytime he wanted to. He had very good rank now and they would get fairly good treatment as to post assignment and occupations. They would think and talk about this more as he was here for a month anyway. Fran was so happy to have him home right now that she was all wiggly and just couldn't sit still. Everyone sat and talked for a time then George asked Fran if she wanted to go with him to see Bob and Bill. Of course she wanted to go, so they started the old car and drove off. George was saying he thought they needed a new car. They pulled into Bill's place and walked up to the door. They had been seen coming and a grand celebration hello was in order. Sandy called Bob and told him to come over with Ann. This now was old home week. Bill couldn't believe that George was here. Bill was really looking good now. Bill told him that Bob was doing very well also. When Bob arrived, Bill made everyone a drink and they sat around and threw the bull. Bob and Bill had kept in touch through the post and they were getting a lot of news. They even heard about George and the line. He had advanced the front line over 50 miles and was awarded the Legion of Merit for this. So he had finally come home. George told them he was only here for a month. Everyone had been hoping the whole mess would have stopped by now.

The three families sat around and talked for hours. This had been a very nice visit and George hated to think of returning back to Korea before long. Bob and Bill were

CHAPTER THIRTEEN

doing fine financially as they had been medically retired from the military. They drew their full pay and could chose between this or a full Veterans Administration retirement. They still maintained their shopping rights on posts also. George told them that he and Fran were looking whether he should stay in after this or get out and see what else might go. He was making fairly good wages now as the top of the hill, a Master Sergeant E-7. He could go no higher but would have fairly good duty from here on. Bob and Bill thought this was really great. The three families agreed to get together next week and have a picnic out by the small lake. So now George and Fran said goodbye and drove back home.

George, Fran and her parents sat in the living room once again. George was interested in Ted's evaluation about his staying in the Army now or getting out. There were jobs out, but most pay was not real good. George's current pay was all right, but the fact of the additional things like housing, shopping privileges and pay increases based on how long you were in the Army. George agreed that many things were possible with the Army, like the war currently going. He had made it this far so he believed he could continue through such things. The news wasn't giving much news anymore about Korea. George and Ted began thinking that things were slowing down substantially there. The hell might be closing down before long. George asked about television stations around close. He was told that Leavenworth had one that would be up and running in another month. This sounded good and George made his mind up instantly. He grabbed everyone and headed to the post. They drove to the PX and headed in to see about a television set. The PX had stocked these things because of the coming station here in town. Kansas City already had two stations up and running. George purchased the monster, a 17-inch Packard Bell. He also needed an antenna for the set. The PX had a man that would come to your house and set this thing up for you. The charge was not bad either. Now George told them they could watch him on television while he was over in Korea. The thing would be installed next week on Wednesday. Ted now was beginning to like the idea. He probably would be able to watch the fights now instead of listening to them on the radio. Ted figured that since the whole family was here now, they should stop by the club and get dinner. This was fine. George drove to the club and they all went inside. The waiter showed them to a table and gave them menus. A bar waiter came around and everyone ordered a drink. Ted of course was well known here. And George was finding out that he was as well. The old salts began stopping by their table and saying hi to Ted and shaking hands with George. His exploits were known around post also. As people came up to speak with Ted, they also noted they had heard about George. Most told Ted it was nice to have a young hero in the family now. Ted was very proud of this and he was really enjoying this evening. The family sat around for a couple hours, and then decided to head for home again.

Ted told Fran that he had known her husband was going to be a good one when he first heard about them. Fran laughed and agreed with her dad. This day had been fantastic, with George seeing so many people he had known. He felt like he had been running around here for the last two weeks. Fortunately he had only been here about two days thus far. Late spring was running very nice now. The weather was typically normal for this time of the year, yielding warm days and cool nights. George was talking with Ted about the winter over there. They had no good winter clothes and most of the guys had suffered frostbite and even more serious problems from the weather. Ted told George he had the same problems in Europe during WWII. He guessed the Army hadn't gained any intelligence about saving soldiers so they could fight better. Ted told George that at times over a third of their units was out because of cold weather problems. Ted told George they needed to go to the post's clothing store to draw warmer things for George before he went back over.

George and Ted were enjoying talking, as both of them knew what the other was saying. You had to be involved in action like this before you could understand any of it. George was learning from Ted and in fact Ted was learning from George about newer problems and actions. Ted did tell George that his wounds and shrapnel would really rear up later in life. You could pick metal out of your body the rest of your left. Finally the girls mentioned that it was about bedtime so everyone needed their rest as they probably would start up in the morning again. So everyone said their goodnights and headed to their separate corners. George was tired from the days running, but he managed to forget this as soon as Fran snuggled up to him. Suddenly George did not care if he got any sleep this night.

The morning came and George and Fran had some rest so they felt good anyway. They got up and dressed and walked upstairs for the breakfast. Ted and Lucy were already up, waiting for the kids to come around. It was only about 7 anyway. No plans had been made for this day so George and Fran thought it might be nice to walk around town. The weather was perfect for this. So a little while after breakfast, they walked out. They met a lot of friends as they

CHAPTER THIRTEEN

walked around. It took about three hours to finish the walk due to everyone wanting to talk. They all thought it was wonderful that George was back for a vacation. When they returned home, they sat in the swing bench on the front porch. They were just enjoying sitting next to each other. They had not exchanged much conversation as yet, but mentally they were both in heaven again. They sat here swinging and getting all the pleasure that was available from a porch swing with your love.

George finally started talking about the Army again. They needed to think out about his re enlistment or getting out completely. The problem was that good jobs were not around too many places. George really did not have any training to offer most places. To be able to get a job with a civilian infantry company was not happening. So they sat and swung and thought. Fran would ask questions every so often. With the military, everyone had free medical also, and if a person was looking at children, this was basically free also. They did not have to make any decision right away, but they both needed to be thinking about this. The couple finally went for another short walk. They moved along arm in arm and soaring in the sky. They returned by early evening and went into the house. Here they sat in the living room and finally Lucy had dinner ready. The family sat around the table and talked about different happenings in the area.

After dinner, Ted and George sat down back in the living room. They were talking about military things again. They always had something to discuss between themselves anyway. A lot of it was without meaning to Fran and Lucy. George was still working on his future career and Ted talked with him. George was really thinking that what he had going with the Army was a lot to throw away. After this war thing in Korea, there was nothing else waiting to start something again that either of them could think of. George wasn't sure how Fran was thinking about this as yet. George's salary now with all the benefits was worth a lot of money. The housing allowance, medical availability, and separate rations were worth a bit of money.

CHAPTER FOURTEEN

George's first week ran by fast. Now the days were beginning to move fast also. Before anything could be planned, it seemed the day was gone already. The main thing was that George was hanging around Fran most of time. The contractor arrived on Wednesday to install the television and antenna. Everyone was really surprised that they were getting Kansas City stations also. So they had television right now with out waiting for the Leavenworth station to come on. On Thursday George and Fran drove out to the small lake with Bill and Bob and their wives. They spread out the blankets and had a nice picnic on the grass by the lake. The weather was perfect for this and the bunch had a blast. George had asked Bill and Bob how their injuries were now.

A CROWN OF GLORY

They both said fine, but there were moments when you would get a reminder about things. Bill had the worst time as his wounds were very serious from the start. Bill did not even miss his lost part of lung. The doctors had all told them they would feel these wound all through life however. George agreed and told them he was having more problems from the shrapnel than anything else. His left leg was somewhat stiff at times. They all agreed that at least they all were alive yet.

The girls wanted to go swimming now. The guys told them go ahead. Of course they did not know the girls had cheated and put suits on under their clothes. There was a loud noise about them cheating. The girls laughed and swam around, close to shore. Finally they climbed out of the water and dried off. Their suits would probably be dry before long also. The guys offered to build a fire and they could take the suits off and they would dry them. This approach failed also. So everyone just sat and waited. The girls seemed to be having a blast with all this fun. Finally the afternoon was coming closer to evening, so the friends all drove back to town. They all figured they needed another of these days before George left again. George and Fran drove back home now and walked in the house. Ted and Lucy were watching the television. This was a neat tool now. Imagine getting a moving picture from the air. Technology was really coming

CHAPTER FOURTEEN

fast now days. George and Fran sat down and watched the thing also.

The days were really moving as George had already found and before long it would be time for him to go back overseas. George and Fran had talked for hours about the Army and so now they had accepted it and would see what happened from here on. When George arrived back in Korea, he would see his Captain about a re enlistment before coming back to the states. He might as well get the time moving for him. As it was, waiting to re-up would start the three years after he was back from over there. If he did it over there, that time would be counted also. George wanted to go to the post tomorrow with Ted and the girls if they wanted to come also. He needed to look into some warmer clothing than he currently had over there. The family watched some television after dinner and found this thing could become habit forming. Everyone had a good day so before long the bed was calling. Every one bid each other a good night and crawled into bed. Tomorrow would be another day. George was pleased the warmer weather was coming on. He wouldn't need the warmer gear now until next fall.

Morning came and everyone was up and ready for the new day. After breakfast, the family loaded up and drove toward Leavenworth. They drove to the clothing store on post and George and Ted began checking over the offerings. It was no wonder that the Army had nothing in Korea, since it was looking as if the stateside units had it all. What George couldn't get issued, he bought. He now had good wool socks and gloves, sweaters, heavy pants and coats. They loaded all this in the trunk and now the girls wanted to stop by the commissary. The girls bought a load of groceries and George paid this time. Next, George needed to check into the transportation section of post regarding his trip back to Korea. He gave them the departure date and they would set something up. He gave them his phone number and they told him they would have the schedule in about two days. So all the days work was finished. The family headed back out to the house.

The next two weeks flashed by and George had his departure information. It would take four to six days for the entire trip. George and Fran lived every moment with each other. There was no idea how long this thing might go on over there. Fran was bracing herself and George was the same way. Fran had cleaned and pressed George's uniform for travel again. The final day finally arrived and the whole family drove into Kansas City for departure from this airport as transportation had arranged. He would fly to Los Angeles, where he would catch a flight to Hawaii. Then it was on hopping across the Pacific until he arrived in Japan. George bid everyone good-bye and he hugged and squeezed Fran until she was almost breathless. He was not sorry for taking this leave as it gave him some more time with his love incase anything bad happened.

George arrived finally in Japan and went to the Korean Military office to get transport on. He was put up in a local barracks for the night and had his last hop in the morning. He began writing a note to Fran already. He was getting back to his old habits. He made it through the night without much sleep and walked to the departure building. This was a smaller plane like a C-47. There were about 30 soldiers heading out. The flight to Korea was not very long and before long they had landed. George climbed down and found a jeep from his rear area waiting for him. He retrieved his bag and climbed on board. They drove off. The driver, a corporal, asked George how the vacation had been. Much too good to be coming back here was his answer. There had not been much action since he had left. Things were just sitting right now. They drove right to the Battalion area and parked. George walked to the orderly room to report in. He was advised the Major wanted to see him right away. George knocked on his door and walked in and reported. The Major was glad to see him. He asked if the leave was good. And he knew it wasn't good to have to come back here. The Major now told George that thanks to George, both he and the Captain were being promoted. The Captain would come up to Battalion and he would go up to Regiment. The Major told him that everything was just sitting right now. There were almost no confrontations along the entire line.

The Major and the Captain had a new position for George if he would take it. He would really not be much good on the line anyway. He was to become the NCOIC of Operational Plans. This was a very busy place and it needed someone just like George, who knew the enemy and his own soldiers and be able to predict what might be coming next. He would have to work right next to the S-2, Intelligence. This almost sounded like some fun to George. He told the Major that he would do the best job he could for him and hoped it would be enough. The Major laughed to told him that he and the Captain had come to the conclusion that George knew what was coming or going by the way his wounds had bothered him. George asked when everyone was moving up. The major told him next week. This sounded very good. George had to get arrangements here now for sleeping and eating. The Battalion had tents and cots to sleep in. Chow was generally served out of the kitchen tent and

CHAPTER FOURTEEN

there were some tables scattered around for everyone's use. Now George found out the Battalion also had laundry service from some local girls. He had a couple of uniforms that could only be thrown away they were so bad. So he found a bunk and there was a hanger type board by the head of the bunks to hang uniforms on.

The Major came around again and got George. He needed to meet the Operations Officer for the Battalion. This man was a major also. He might be in line to take the battalion over when the other Major went up to Regiment. This Major shook George's hand and told him he had heard some fantastic stories about him. Well, George's new position was looking good anyway. There wasn't very many times a rear echelon unit had been overrun. At least you could generally walk around without worry about a sniper shooting at you. George looked around and finally found his desk with his own nametag on it. This tent was the Operations tent. So George settled in and began learning what he was to do. He would be required to travel up to the front now and then to check on things. His abilities here were a key to creating this position. He would be the key to the Operational Officers arrangements. So here was the new horizon for George's military career.

A CROWN OF GLORY

George sat down at his desk and started looking over papers in his in box. He found a lot of information that he did not know. There were peace talks going on but nothing was looking like any change in the near future. One paper was listing the different units that were holding the line on this side. The Battalion was wondering about moving the line forward in the near future. George knew how to get this started. He wrote a DF form to the Operations Officer. He recommended that each company on line start moving patrols out during the daytime and look for enemy activity. George had a much better picture of the line now with all the maps here. The enemy had been in somewhat of a retreat from the current line. George was thinking this might be from a hard supply option. The enemy was far from their normal areas, and supply for them required hand packing and what vehicles they could get toward their front. His figured that the supply was the main thing that was hindering the enemy from moving on down more. As the 'good guys' were just sitting and not getting anywhere, the enemy was probably just sitting also and waiting until their supply line began working again. So now was the time to strike forward. He hoped the patrols might tell what everyone was doing. The Operations Officer forwarded his orders to the line. By morning, George should know what was really going on. He could see on the map that the enemy might be willing a ease off this front for another 20 kilometers. At this point, his supply would be catching up by now. The secret probably would have to be a steady onward trek toward northern property.

George had a young private assigned to his section. This man could type and keep files for the unit. This would help a lot, as George was more an action man than an office sitter. As soon as they heard back from the companies on line, then he would probably run up and look the area over. George's whole plan now would lean on the information between the companies and his personal view of the area. This was interesting and he really hoped he wouldn't mess things up. George needed to find out from the Operations Officer what the latest intelligence he had been given. He had looked through most of his in box and he was beginning to get the idea of what his job might be. Everyone would soon find out if his ideas about the line might be true. If not, he would have to work up better information from current reports from the front and the latest intelligence. George had met the Battalion Master Sergeant and he seemed like a nice guy. He had been in for almost 18 years and was from WWII also. George walked over to his office and checked if he had any of the information that he would like to get. Frank, the Master

A CROWN OF GLORY

Sergeant, was working yet. George talked with him some and Frank invited him to come around after chow. He had a bottle and they could have a drink if he wanted. George liked this and the whole organization down here. You could learn a lot after being around here for only a couple of days.

CHAPTER FIFTEEN

orning rolled around and George was up and going early. He hoped this day would bring him information regarding his plans. He should hear something by mid afternoon from the front. Frank and George had talked some last night and Frank seemed to like this new idea about thinking ahead of the enemy. The two had talked for about three hours last night and George had learned many interesting things about this unit here. Most of the new information was normal, but some would guide George in the future toward getting certain things approved faster. George believed one of the problems back here was the slow motion that everyone seemed to run on. When news was heard that was important and useable for helping on the line, it needed to be transmitted to the line in one way or another. The Operations Officer called for George and told him his idea about patrols had been given the go ahead and the line units should be out right now. This was very good. Now George wanted to push another helpful idea for the front. He wanted at least a battery of 155 howitzers to be moved close enough to be able to support the patrols that needed to be sent out a lot more. When the front was getting no action, there was either something coming up or the enemy was back and looking at another area. George figured if the battery could move within two or three kilometers of the rear Battalion here, they could be of much more use. As everyone moved forward, they should also. The Operations Officer liked this plan also and told George he would get right on it.

The change within the battalion was beginning now. The Operations Officer was moving up to become the Commanding Officer. The Captain from the line, now a Major, moved up to become the Operations Officer. George liked this. He and the Major had always got along well. By afternoon, the patrols were checking in. No sign of enemy anywhere over the next four kilometers. This was as George had suspected. George now asked the new Major if he could go forward and look around the front line. The permission was granted so George obtained a jeep and drove off. He

CHAPTER FIFTEEN

stopped and talked to each company and to the patrol units. He was getting the whole thing now and could see out front. This seemed to be just as he had figured. George drove back to the rear and told his Major that the line needed to be moved maybe four kilometers ahead. After this, they needed to continue patrol checks if they had no contact with the enemy yet. The orders were given and the line moved forward. By this time, the front did not bother to dig elaborate foxholes. They made just enough cover to get protection. The next morning the patrols were off once again. With the reports in, the line was told to move forward the next day by five Kilometers. Now the Battalion had to be moved and the battery of 155's. George was turning this war in a motion one. The old Army saying of 'move, shoot, and communicate' was the name of the current game. In three days, the line had moved 9 kilometers forward.

The rear Regiment headquarters was wondering what the hell was going on up at this battalion. The information was called back to them and they understood. George was back in making things happen. Now the regiment had to pass this information on to the rest of their front line. Very soon the whole front was moving rapidly forward. Over the next week, the front line had gained another 30 kilometers forward. By this time, the Army commander, General

Grisson was wondering what was going on. As the information trickled forward, he could see the situation. General Grisson drove up to the Battalion headquarters to meet this Master Sergeant who was bringing all this around. He was amazed seeing such a young man in this position. He went to the battalion's commander and asked some questions. Now things were coming around. This was the man who had been wounded so many times they had been talking about giving him a medical credit card. He also was the one that advanced the front 50 miles in the past. The General told the Major that if he had three more men like this, he could probably win the war in a week and a half.

George now had the General's eye and anything he asked for, he got. George finally got the line ahead for a total of 60 kilometers. Now he sat down and told the units to dig in for a stay. George figured that the enemy would be seeing the creeping front line and decide to get back into combat. All the rear headquarters were moved along with the front. They now had more troops in reserve also. The regiment was ready for a new war. George's Major was biting his fingernails and worrying about the front line. George told him there would be some new hard combat within 48 hours on the front. They needed to get plenty of ammo up front and support supply areas running. The batteries of 155's needed to make sure they had more than enough rounds also. For every battalion on the line, he wanted one on reserve to help them. There was much running around and soon commanders in the rear began questioning George's knowledge. The General put a stop to this immediately.

As if on cue, the second day began with a full frontal assault on the front line. There seemed to be a massive amount of troops coming south now. The fighting was like some of the first here, but this time the units had ammo and support behind them. The massive assault continued for almost a week. Then it began to trickle down until there was almost nothing going on. Soon intelligence was getting word that over an entire Army had been destroyed and the enemy supply line had given out again. The General came by again. He had been asking his commanders in the rear why they hadn't figured things out like this Master Sergeant could. The General sat and talked with George for over an hour. George told him how he had learned to read the enemy and that it had worked very well. The General asked George to come with him and have lunch. So George went. He felt as if he was on display sitting with the General and chatting. They even were laughing at times and they looked as if they were just old friends. After lunch, the two walked back toward Georges office tent. The General stopped by his jeep and grabbed a bottle. At the office, the General presented this bottle to George. It was a fine bottle of the best scotch. George asked if he wanted a drink, but the General refused and told George this was all his, a special thanks from him. The General said goodbye and told George he would be around later again. George thanked him and returned to his desk after the General left.

The General wasn't gone for five minutes before everyone was in George's Office asking questions. Most were officers and a few enlisted. Everyone had seen them at lunch and wondered if George had known him from the past. No, George had just met him in Korea here. One thing anyway, no one wanted to make any waves to or about George now. George got back to work and wanted some new patrol information. This time, he only wanted one patrol per company and then only from three different companies along the line. He had a funny feeling that something had been left uncovered out there. The next morning he received the news that the patrol had entered into combat about 2 kilometers in front of the line. He had this opinion and was glad he had been conservative. He would wait now for another day and if no other contact was made, then it would be time to send out the regular patrols again. George was thinking that maybe he should drive up to the front again and take a look for

CHAPTER FIFTEEN

himself. He drove up and talked with various Company commanders and senior enlisted men. This gave him information along the lines he was looking for. He talked to the patrol members on the last patrol and heard some additional information that had not been sent back. The patrols had hardly seen any enemy, just started getting fire toward them. This could have been only a small group of enemy, maybe 3 to 5 men. George was getting information that was extremely valuable. This information did not come with written reports or radio messages. George finally thanked everyone and drove back to the battalion area.

George next began going through intelligence reports that had been sent to operations. He was seeing many things that did not seem right. He was totally baffled right now. He walked to the S-2, Intelligence section. He talked with the captain there and a couple of sergeants. Once again, George was seeing that the real message was not getting into the written reports of things. The originators of these various reports were only reporting what was known to be exactly true. Much of the information was being missed because of this. A person could see a soda bottle out on patrol and think it might have been a soldier's drink, but this information never got into any report. He needed to sit down with his Major and the Battalion Commander to discuss this information. The rear areas needed exact information about patrols and visual pictures. The commander agreed and would get an order out immediately. George told him he needed to inform all his people here of the same information.

George next wanted to get another patrol out just like the ones yesterday and see what their reports might show in the next afternoon. George had a plan but he was not saying anything at present. He was thinking the enemy was pulling back as maybe the talks in Paris were getting closer. He figured the troops would hold very small pockets to seem like an enemy position. This now could be a waiting game. The current front line was about to the middle line that had separated Korea in the past. George would really like to know what was actually going on at the peace talks. He wasn't sure and there probably was no one around here that would know either. So George would just have to wait and try to guess daily. The patrols were going to be invaluable for information now. He just hoped he could read the information correctly. George next sat down with his Major and discussed with him what he thought was happening. The Major believed that George had fairly well figured the situation out. But they both agreed to run softly for now. Tomorrows' reports might show something else yet.

CHAPTER FIFTEEN

George walked out to the benches by the tables and sat down. He was deep in thoughts and needed this get away thing. He sat here thinking and before long, the time for supper had arrived. George ate and then walked down the road for a way. He could not get his mind clear of this front line problem. There must be something that he was not really seeing. George walked back and went to his barracks tent. He lie down on his bunk and shortly fell off to sleep. He had not been sleeping very well due to all the action around. He must have been very tired as he was sleeping soundly. About three in the morning, George jerked awake with a start. He had been dreaming while he slept and suddenly his dream had shown him what was going on. His dream was about the 'Trojan' horse in a fable about old time warfare a long time back. This dream was the answer for George anyway about the current affairs. He jumped up and ran to his desk and began writing and studying the map. The enemy here was using their own special Trojan horse. The small groups of enemy found every now and then was to develop the front lines thinking to believe they were still interested in this territory. While everyone was pissing around with this, they would move around on the edges of the front and get a large enough unit of soldiers to attack in the rear of the front line. This was the answer. George ran to the control room and grabbed the NCO on duty. He told him to wake everyone involved with operations and intelligence here. He told him to get the Commander up also. This could be life or death.

It was almost 5 now and blurry-eyed men were stumbling out of their beds and coming to the Operations section. Here, George had set up a control point for right now. As the men came into the tent, they did not look real happy and most had been long gone into dreamland. Once everyone was here, George apologized for dragging everyone up but this was a most important thing. He explained what the enemy had been working after he had found out from talking with the men on patrol directly. It looked like they were leaving a very small group every so often, to hide and open up fully on a patrol like a larger force. This was the bait they hoped to make the US believe they were still working this area strong and in some force. This was enacted to guide the US into a lulled sense of peace with no strong action against the front line. This was working very well. Now George told about the Trojan horse and everyone remembered the story. Well these small groups of enemy were their Trojan horse. While the US was concentrating on these small clashes, the main force of the enemy would be working around the edge of the front line. They would concentrate forces to the outside and behind areas of the

CHAPTER FIFTEEN

front line. When the units were still sound asleep, they could get into position and attack from the rear. This would involve rear units as well. George now drug out the maps. He indicated a perfect area to the left rear of the front line, where the enemy could concentrate a large force and not be found, at least very easy. George needed the commanders to direct every free unit to this location and pull at least half the men off the front line as it was right now. There was some grumbling about this and the battalion commander said flat out that the regiment would never go along with this. George advised them if they didn't like it talk with the General. This sealed all loopholes now.

The Regiment was told about the plan and would precede but if this were a fake plan, George would be held accountable. The available troops were headed toward the target area and artillery batteries were told to plan locations where they could reach need targets in the area. A temporary command location was plotted and everything was in high gear. It took over a day to get into positions for everyone. Once it was in place, the mass of troops began moving slowly forward. Within 5 kilometers of the start, the enemy was caught flat out with no advance guards and no real support from their rear echelon. The enemy was caught in a slaughter by the UN forces. Over the next two days, intelligence figured that another Army from the north was destroyed. After a mop up of the operations, the UN forces returned to their old positions. George returned to his position with Battalion and he relaxed once again. Thank God for that silly dream. George hadn't been back for three hours when here came the General. He went straight to George's tent. He slapped George on the back and told him if it were in his power, he would make George a general right now. He did offer him a combat commission, but George turned him down saying his education wasn't that good. The General told him if he ever wanted it just let him known. George had pulled the troops out of harms way once again.

CHAPTER SIXTEEN

The front line was now doing nothing, as there currently was no enemy around to fight. Regiment talked with George and agreed to move the line up to the exact line that had been used to separate north and south. Now this was to become a waiting game. The word kept coming down that the talks were going well and this mess should be over in a very few days. Everyone sat and waited. George wanted to get back home. He was very tired of this stupid war and could really not understand why everyone was stopped at this location. He wanted to get back to his family and begin enjoying normal life again. The word finally came down that the UN police action was finished. There would be a controlling force maintained here. All soldiers that had been over here from the start were being sent home. New men would begin the control force. The General came down to Battalion and talked with George again. He had been very proud that his regiment had this man. The general finally asked George if he would fly home with him. George thought this would be very nice and thanked the General. The General had a jeep come for George a couple of days later and load his gear up in the jeep. George was still opening eyes around. He bid the Battalion farewell and rode off. The General had pinned another star on over here and he blamed George. George had eased a lot of promotions through, but he was as high as he could go unless he wanted the commission. He was sure this would not work for him so he was happy to sit where he was. The General had a nice assigned plane. It was a DC-6, a four-engine plane that could hold a lot of people. There were quite a few people on board also.

George arrived with the General and they sat in an office type room up front. This was impressive and the engines cranked up. This trip would take somewhere around two to three days. The general was traveling back to Fort Leavenworth where he would be assigned as the Commander for the War College there. George smiled and told the General that his family was around there and he was

CHAPTER SIXTEEN

returning to be assigned at Fort Leavenworth also. The General did not seem surprised. George got a funny thought now. He was sure the General had stepped in and made this assignment. The General talked with George most of the time. The General wanted to know where George had studied tactics for war. This almost surprised George. He told the General that he had not studied this it was plain common sense. They both laughed at this and the General was even more amazed. The General now decided to play some games. He had his aid bring out some maps and an easel for them. He began by giving George a situation on the map and asked George to plan a battle. George liked this. He looked the map over and asked a couple of questions. He studied the map for about 15 minutes and then told the General what would be a course of action to come out ahead in the battle. The General just shook his head and was amazed. The battle had been an actual one during WWII. The top commanders had led the plan of action. They took a month to get up with this plan that would work. George had done it in a few minutes. Now the General wanted another one, so the game went on. Each plan, George had given the correct answer in only a few minutes, versus days and weeks it had taken the top Generals to figure out.

A CROWN OF GLORY

The General wanted George to take a position at the War College and teach for him. George told him that he had no education for teaching. The General laughed and told George if this was the key, then the whole world needed a lot of uneducated men if this was the result. The General was serious about George teaching however. He told George that he would have a very easy schedule and probably only work three to four days a week. He couldn't promote George but anything he could do he would. The General now informed George that he was getting a personal Presidential Citation for his work in Korea. He probably would have to fly to Washington to get it. The President wanted to present this himself. George finally accepted the General's position at the War College. He wondered what Ted would say about this.

The plane ride was up and down. They would fly about 15 hours and land to get some rest. They took off again in a few hours and after a meal, and rode some more. It took a full three days to get to Kansas City. There, the General had a car waiting for him. George was asked to ride with him to Leavenworth. George thanked him and told the General he could call his family from there to get a ride out to home. The General refused to hear this. This car would take him clear home. At Fort Leavenworth, the General got out and told George to call him in a couple of weeks. George thanked the General and the car took him on toward home. It was late afternoon when George pulled up in front of the house. He saw everyone looking out the window and when they figured out who this was, they all came running out. The driver opened the trunk and got George's baggage. George thanked the driver and he left. Ted asked how he managed to get a staff car to bring him out. George smiled and told him it was the General's car and when they had dropped him off in Leavenworth, the driver was told to take George home. Now Ted was really interested. George told Ted about riding with the General all the way from Korea. And he was to be assigned to the War College as an instructor. George now told them he was going to fly to Washington as the President wanted to present him with a special Presidential Citation for his work in Korea.

This was a load of news, but Fran didn't really care. She had George back again and she was very happy. They sat in the living room for a while talking. The Korean mess was over for now and everyone including George was very glad to be back home, safe and sound. The family had sat around for about 30 minutes and now George wanted to get out of this uniform he had worn for the last three days. He excused himself and headed down stairs. Fran giggled and winked at her parents. Down she ran after George. Ted was wondering just what George had been doing. He could see some long talks coming in the future. Ted knew about the War College and had seen the building, but he really never knew what things were taught there. It did appear that George had been charging straight forward just like he did around here. His daughter could have done a lot worse and he was glad that he and Lucy had pushed things for this match up. Ted was thinking of taking the kids out for dinner. Lucy thought this might be nice also. When the kids came back up they were asked if it was ok to go out for dinner. This was fine for them. So everyone climbed into Ted's car and they headed out for dinner. Ted figured the club on post would be good and they drove there. They were taken to a table as usual and they ordered drinks. Next the food menus were scanned and they ordered a meal. The club was quiet and peaceful so far tonight. Of course the normal crowd of men who knew Ted began stopping by and speaking. The four just sat and sipped their drinks. Before long they would be happy and secure with their family again.

The meals came and everyone was hungry. They enjoyed the meal and was just happily sitting around and enjoying an after dinner drink. A man walked up in civilian clothes and said hi to George. George stood up and greeted the General. He then introduced Ted and the Girls. The

CHAPTER SIXTEEN

General was pleased to meet them. He also knew of Ted very well, and the General told him it was always nice to meet a Medal of Honor man. He mentioned that some of that must have brushed off on George. The General next excused himself and walked toward the office. Ted looked at George and then asked him if this was the General he had traveled with. George told him it was. Things slid into place now for Ted. His son-in-law was rubbing with the big boys. The family finished with their drinks and they decided to go home. It had been a long day for everyone by now.

George and Fran went downstairs and fell into bed. They didn't get back up until around 8 the next morning. Ted and Lucy had eaten but Lucy was waiting for the kids to cook something for them. George felt a lot better this morning. He was ready to relax and rest up now for months. The family happily chatted about what had gone on around here. George was very closed mouthed about Korea. He didn't say much except it was a war and very dangerous. Many of his old friends had not made the grade to come back alive. Ted understood this as much as anyone. A person has to go through combat before you can really know what goes on. Over the next two weeks, George and Fran had visited with Bob, Ann, Bill, and Sandy. They now could see a good future relationship with old friends. George and Fran did see others that they had missed during the last two years. The middle of the third week, the General had called for George. He wanted him to come in and look around. So George put on his uniform and drove to the post. He walked in the War College and a person at the front desk took him to the General's office. Here they sat and talked some. He finally took George on a grand tour of the college building. He showed George an office on the main floor that was to be his. This was building into a very big and strange occupation.

George and the General returned to his office. He wanted George to start as soon as he returned from Washington. George asked when he would be going there and the General told him on Thursday. This would be good since George could make arrangement and let his family know. The General told George that his family was going along with him. They were to be guests at the White House. Their tickets were already obtained and the General gave them to George. He told George that a Limo would pick the family up and drive them to Kansas City and to the plane. It would also be there to pick them up. When the family arrived in Washington, the White House would have a car waiting for them there. Everything had been figured down to the last nail. The General now double-checked that George's family was four people. This was correct George told him.

CHAPTER SIXTEEN

The General thanked George for coming in and wished him a very nice trip.

George drove home, still a little confused. This new job might be good and it might be bad, probably depending on how a person looked at it. He was having trouble understanding why he was being called to the White House. Most medals were presented at the soldier's home post. Well, it should be interesting going to the White House anyway. George drove up in front of the house and got out. He walked in the house and announced the family was going on a short vacation. Now everyone was all ears. George informed them the government was flying them all to Washington. There a limo from the White House would pick them up and drive them to the White House, where they were to be guests. Everyone's jaw dropped on this. George told them they were leaving tomorrow early afternoon. He hoped no one had anything important planned. A thousand questions started now. George couldn't answer most of them. He had been asking himself about the same questions and had no answer.

George asked Fran about his dress class A uniform and if it was clean and pressed. She told him it was. He had been told this was almost required on this coming Friday. The family did what planning they needed and withdrew some money from the bank. They packed smaller suitcases for a shorter stay as they had been advised. Ted took a suit and also his dress class A uniform, just in case. He was proud of his service and that of his son-in-law. The girls checked everything about ten times and they were running around almost dangerously. At least now there was a whole bunch of excitement within the family.

CHAPTER SEVENTEEN

The day came and everyone was waiting for the limo to arrive. It was scheduled for 10. The time came and it arrived. The driver helped with the suitcases and opened doors for the ladies at the minimum. He drove out of town and headed toward Kansas City. The Limo drove to a gate at the airport. It was not going to the regular passenger terminal and the family was confused. The limo driver knew where he was going and he pulled up next to an Air Force DC-6 airplane. The driver helped the girls out and headed up the steps into the plane. He next grabbed the luggage and gave this to one of the crewmen on the plane. The plane was very nice on the inside. It was not the run of the mill Air Force plane. The passenger aid on board was a man. He helped the family into their seats and the plane started its engines.   It wasn't very long until they were flying high. The passenger aid now asked if anyone would like a drink.   They all agreed and he served them drinks. Not bad for an Air Force plane. The trip took almost four hours and when they landed in Washington, there was a limo at the area. The passenger aid helped the girls down to the ground and handed the suitcases to the limo driver. They were loaded up and drove off into Washington.

The limo pulled right up into the White House grounds and parked by a side door. Here a man was waiting for them and showed them to their rooms. He told them after they had freshened up he would take them to the dinning room for dinner. The family thanked the man and relaxed in their rooms. This was a whole different activity than any of them had ever been involved with. About an hour and a half, the man came around and asked if they were ready for dinner. This was fine. The man led them to the dinning room that appeared to be able to seat about 200 people at individual tables. He gave them what was a short menu and asked about a drink. He took these orders and served the drinks. He returned shortly to see if they were ready to order. The family gave him their orders. The meal was served them and then the waiter asked about an after dinner drink. This sounded fine to the family also, so the waiter brought these. When the whole dinner was over, the man came over to the table and thanked them for coming. He would accept no tip. He also told them there would a man coming to see them in a moment.

Shortly a man approached the family and asked them to follow him. The family followed the man and he took them to a large sitting room. The man told them to wait for a minute and the President would be in. This was really something. Shortly again, a door opened and the President stepped in. The family stood up and the President shook hands with everyone, calling them by name. He asked them all to sit. He wanted to talk with them for a little while. He now told them that he wanted to see and speak with them before tomorrow. He had been given certain information from a man who had been his aid during WWII. This man was now George's General. There was the connection. The President asked George about some things attributed to him. George told him that many people were involved in these things. He was not responsible for the outcomes. The President nodded his head and smiled. He told the family that this comment he had expected. He would have been disappointed if George had said anything else. Now he was sure about the information. They all talked for about an hour and the President mentioned to Ted that he had been the one that had pinned the Congressional Medal of Honor medal on him in Europe. Ted had not forgotten, but figured the President would have by now. The President told them that any thing so important to the nation and to him could never be forgotten. He stood up now and excused himself. He was sorry but he had some things to do yet tonight. He asked Ted and George to wear their uniforms tomorrow if they could. They agreed. The President left and the other man came back in to escort them to their quarters again.

The family was astounded by these events. It didn't seem possible to be here and to have talked with the President. They all were so up that sleep was not an option right now. A knock came at the door. George answered and it was a man who handed him some papers. This would be for the next day, a schedule of sorts. The family sat down and looked the information over. There was almost a step by step procedure to be followed and almost by the minute it looked like. The family finally decided to crawl in bed as the morning looked as if it might be a flurry of action around here. The rooms had television set in each. George turned the set on and surprised at the good signal here. He left the set on with low volume and crawled into bed. The entire family slept on and off all night. At 6 in the morning, they received a wake up call. They were given an hour to get ready for breakfast. The information they received last night asked that the men not dress in their uniforms yet. At 7, they were escorted to breakfast. The same dinning room was used and now there were a few other people eating in here. At 8:30, they were escorted to another room and a guide appeared to give them a tour of the White House. This would be fantastic. The tour took up almost 2 hours and it was very nice to see all the things everyone heard about but very seldom got to see. They were now taken to another room and served coffee. They were asked to stay here for a few minutes and a man would come to orient them for the afternoon. About 11 a man entered the room and introduced himself. He was one of the assistants to the President. He now explained the plan for this afternoon. After the family ate lunch, they needed to go to their rooms and change into their uniforms for the ceremony. This man ran them through what would be done during the ceremony. He advised them regarding their places on the stage with the President. This was really getting big now. The man talked to the family until about 11:30 and then bid them good day. They would be escorted from their rooms after lunch to the area the ceremony was to take place.

A CROWN OF GLORY

The family was led to the dinning room once again and they ordered a light lunch. From here, they were taken back to their rooms. Here the men changed into their uniforms, and the girls changed into their best cloths. They sat in their rooms now and awaited the escort. Shortly, a man came by and asked them to follow him. He led them to a smaller room with a door going to what appeared the outside. Here the family would come out on the top of the steps and take their positions. As soon as they had, the President would come out. There was a large crowd outside and the family was getting somewhat afraid. The man here opened the door and told the family to get into their positions. The President was just coming into this room. He followed them outside on the top of the stairs. The President began speaking through the public address system out here. He rambled on about the recent police action in Korea and even back to WWII. Finally, he mentioned that the military men were what made this country great. He introduced George first, telling the crowd what he had given up and how he all but won the action at least for the United States. The crowd clapped and George stepped forward as he had been instructed. The President held a ribbon and medal and told everyone that this was his highest medal with only the Congressional Medal of Honor higher. He told Master Sergeant George Franklin he was awarding him this personal Presidential Citation award for his untold and exceptional bravery while in Korea, saving hundreds of lives. He pinned the medal on George's uniform and George came to attention and saluted the President. He stepped back to his position. Now the President presented Ted to the crowd. He was George's father-in-law and he had been awarded with the Congressional Medal of Honor in the last war. This award had been presented by this President back then. The crowd was really sucking up this event. Now the President had his words to say about the wives. He told the crowd that these women were the ones who had to wait at home and wonder if they would ever see their husbands again. They were the core of America with their strong stance beside their husbands. Everyone clapped again. The President now dismissed the ceremony and as more pictures were being flashed, he and the family left the stage. Once inside, the President thanked the family for coming and wished them the best of luck in the future. He walked through a door and a man came in to escort them back to their rooms.

This had been a high energy-eating day so far. George lay on the bed and relaxed. He must have fallen asleep since he awoke to a knock on the door. The man advised them that dinner would be served very soon. The family got up and walked toward the dinning room. The men still wore their uniforms. They came to the dinning room and a man met them at the door. He asked them to follow him. He took them through the large dinning room and into a smaller room with a table. It was set and the man asked the family to sit down. He told them the President would be with them shortly. They only had to wait about four minutes when the President entered with his wife. The family stood up and the President thanked them but asked them to sit. This would be one of the special times he would be informal. He had ordered for everyone if this was all right. Drinks were brought as usual, this time following what the family had last night. A few minutes after this, a grand meal was served. It was a lavish five course meal and top quality all the way. The President and his wife just sat here and chatted with everybody. She seemed to be having fun also. The President began asking some questions about Georges military career. He told the President that he was going to stay in now that he had the rough points from war rounded off. The President laughed, as did his wife. The President told George that his former aid, the General had told him about George and his tactic knowledge and that George had been offered a direct commission but turned it down. George laughed and told the President he would be one of the most ignorant officers in his

CHAPTER SEVENTEEN

Army if he took the commission. The President laughed and said that he figured he had a large amount of these already. The President told George that the smartest thing the General had ever done was to assign George to the War College. Maybe he could teach some of the officers how to figure tactics.

The dinner became very enjoyable with the President and his wife. The President told them it was refreshing to sit down with some real heroes. His medals had basically come from the men he led. The two families sat and talked for quite awhile and everyone was enjoying this dinner. The President told George he would be watching him and after he was out of office, he would pass this on to the next President. Men like George and Ted did not grow on trees and the country needed to see them and thank them everyday. Everyone was stuffed after the dinner and now they sat with an after dinner drink and talked longer. Finally, the President was called out. He bid the family good bye and apologized for leaving them. The First Lady also got up to go. She thanked everyone for the delightful dinner. She told them they didn't get too many of these anymore. It had been very refreshing to sit down with good home-grown people. A few minutes later, a man entered the room and escorted them to their rooms for the night.

A CROWN OF GLORY

The family sat together in one room for a while. They had really seen about everything now. They turned on the television set and the news was on. Here it showed the ceremony for this day and what the President had said. It showed the hundreds of people that were around the grounds at the White House. Well if anyone needed to know whom any of this family was, they would surely know by now. The family sat around and talked for quite a while. Their schedule for tomorrow had them leaving here and being transported back to the airport. They would catch the flight back to Kansas City and get on home. This had been an experience of a lifetime and things now would be a slow down for the family.

CHAPTER EIGHTEEN

The morning came and the family was up getting ready for the new day. They had breakfast and a different man approached them and gave them some photos for them to keep. These photo's were of the ceremony, but then a few photo's were showing them eating with the President last night. They had been unaware of any pictures being taken. The note with these pictures was from the President. He was thanking them for the most enjoyable dinner he had been at for a very long time. The family finished breakfast and they went back to their rooms and began collecting their personals and packing up the suitcases. Their plane was due to leave about 10. The limo came around for them and a man helped them out to the vehicle and put their suitcases in the trunk. They were driven away toward the airport. They arrived here and basically had a reverse trip from the one coming. They arrived in Kansas City around 2. The limo was waiting here also and drove them home. This had been a rapid vacation and a whole lot to remember. They were ready to get home and collapse for some good rest. This was evidently not in the cards right now. Friends and neighbors surrounded their house. Well this would take a while to get everyone's imagination brought back down. The limo pulled up and the driver helped the girls out and then retrieved the suitcases from the trunk. He took them and set them just inside the house. The mob was on everyone. Some had seen the television broadcast of the ceremony. This had been the talk of the entire town. Everyone wanted the fine details about their visit. When they showed them having dinner with the President and his wife, this smashed everyone. The crowd finally had seen everything and about heard all the minute by minute details so the family told them bye and ran into their house.

Home now, they collapsed and relaxed in the living room. Ted turned the television on to see if there were any fights or such on. Nothing but an announcement about what had happened yesterday at the White House. Great, this was still going around here. George nodded his head down and was almost asleep. Fran nudged him and giggled as she always did. She must have been getting relaxed before anyone else. George was off until at least Monday now. He would have to call in during the weekend to see if he was scheduled for anything. He was willing to try this new duty but he wasn't sure how he would do. The family now had all weekend to rest up, if everyone would leave them alone. If not, then it would have to attend to getting quiet time in other places. The family tried to be hidden and not go outside where other people could see them. It was almost as bad as being in a security section of a jail. Everyone hoped things would get calm before long.

George awoke Saturday morning and called in to see if he had anything going Monday. The CQ greeted him and told him he had seen the family on television. That was real neat. He also told George that he had a book waiting here for him to study and a few notes. So George agreed he would come in and get things today. The family decided they would go along as they could at least get out of the house for a time. They drove to the post and George walked into the War College. He was greeted by security here and told to go to the CQ's office. He knew this. He came to the office and the CQ gave him his things. He welcomed George to the War College and told him it was a great place to work. George walked back to the car and was looking at the book. It was a book about bad battle decisions man had made through the ages. There were a lot of notes from the General also. One told him to not worry about coming in until the next week. He had seen the television show of the ceremony at the White House and knew this would wear a person down. After this, the family thought a drive might be nice. They could drive a few miles and get some lunch where people wouldn't recognize them.

They headed out to the south and drove about 40 miles. There was a small café among some other buildings so the family decided to get a bite here. They parked and walked into the café and found a booth. The waitress came by with water and menus. She walked back to the kitchen. Everyone was reading the menu and figuring what they wanted to eat. A man with the waitress came out and asked if he could get a picture of our group. He wanted to hang it on the wall. No one famous ever came by here. The family laughed and agreed to the picture. They told the man they really weren't famous however. He told them he had watched the program on television yesterday. The family ate their orders and paid and left, thinking there was no safe spot anymore. They drove back home and camped down in the house once again. Bob called later and asked if the famous people would agree to visitors tomorrow. Fran laughed so they said they would come over in the afternoon to see everyone again. They would probably have Bill and his wife with them also.

The days now began to pass at a more normal speed. Before George knew, it was time to go to work. Fran had washed and pressed his dress uniforms and he headed toward the War College. It might be interesting to see how this building ran and worked. George went to his office and began looking over his in basket. He was running through things when the General walked in. George jumped up and the General told him at ease. The General was glad to see him at work finally. He asked about the book and George told him he might understand how civilization had taken so long to gain much. George had read about many of these battles, however they were not shown in so bad a light. The General asked how George found the President. He had been in total awe of the whole trip. And he did not know that the General had been an aid to him during war. The General grinned and told him this information was not general public knowledge, especially at this date. The General now wanted to assign a class to George. He gave him the class of values about the first Roman attack into German held territory.

George had always been interested in this battle. The General asked about the next battle George liked. He mentioned the Battle of Agincourt in the 15th century between France and England. The General was impressed. These would be the two Battles that George would talk about this week. The General asked George to not practice his class delivery. He wanted George just like he was with no fancy classroom performance. George told him this was fine with him. The General left now telling George his first class was next hour in room 214. He also asked George to act as if the class were six year olds in public school. George thought and agreed that many officers were really in this group.

George walked up to room 214 and found it empty right now. He walked in and set the general room up, as he wanted it to be. He next wrote his name on the chalkboard along with the title of this class. He sat down with some of his papers and set his mind into the Battle between Germans and Romans. He had studied this a lot since it was very much like the War of Independence in 1776. 11 O'clock rolled around and the classroom began to fill up. The class was made up of mainly Majors, Captains, and a couple of Lt. Colonels. At the start time, George introduced himself and began the class. His first part was to give the class a scenario of the pre battle lay out. Next George asked students how they might begin moving to the battle area. Most, knowing how strong the Roman army was, elected to charge straight into the German stronghold. The students were allowed to inject their thoughts now about this general method. Now George began diagramming the first part of the battle on the chalkboard. He began showing what the German hill men had been doing most of their lives. The Roman commander had not studied the enemy and had very little information about the enemy before entering into the battle. The Germans were used to fighting from protected areas and were acting much like the early Americans during the War of Independence. The Romans were used to fighting face to face with their enemy and had one of the best armies ever conceived for this type of fighting. George showed how the Roman commander had acted even after seeing the Germans fight. The Roman had been unable to change his tactics in the middle of a battle. This was a major point that George pushed to the class. A commander has to be able to adjust and change his tactics at all times during an ongoing battle. When the class was dismissed, several officers came up and told George he had a very good class. Many of them had already learned about George and were proud to have him as an instructor.

George erased the chalkboard and walked down to his office. The General was waiting for him. All the classrooms had monitors, which allowed certain people to listen to the class in progress. The General had been impressed with George's first class. He had already received some outstanding comments from some of the students. They seemed to think the college here was finally getting some instructors that really knew what they were talking about. The General told George his next class was scheduled for Thursday and was regarding the Battle of Agincourt in 1415. This was another of George's favorite historic battles. So George began his new career as an instructor. He was enjoying the duty and the War College had benefited huge amounts by putting him in such a position.

CHAPTER NINETEEN

Time passed on and George and Fran bought a house around the small town where her parents and their friends were. They brought a couple of children in the world, a boy named George Jr., and a girl named Tracy. They were leading a fairly nice life now. George was more or less permanent in his assignment as an instructor at the War College. Some years later, the Army approved the addition of new super grades for the enlisted men. George was one of the first to be raised to the rank of Master Sergeant E-8. The army also had a Sergeant Major E-9. George and Fran walked through the life with George in the Army and the children in local schools. They both had seen their entire career would be spent here at Ft. Leavenworth. The General moved on to become a top ranking General covering over half the United States in regards to the military there. Many of the student officers at the War College continued to send George notes and clippings about their careers with the Army. It was rather nice to keep track of all these men. Things were still going very well and George had become thoroughly set in his spot at the War College. There had been minor combat situations around the world, but George had been not been called. There began to be rumors about a small Indochina country having problems. This was a civil war between a communist government and a democratic seeking one. The country, Vietnam, had been little known in the past. The United States began watching this civil war and when asked they sent some troops in to help train southern army. This had only amounted to about 500 army personnel.

George continued teaching and now began looking at some of the jungle battles that this country of Vietnam was having. This country had been fighting among themselves for hundreds of years. During the present problems, China had stepped in to assist the northern communist group. The art of the jungle fighting communists was a new type of warfare. Most of it was hit and run tactics and it reminded George of the battle between the Romans and the German hill people.

CHAPTER NINETEEN

History has recorded many types of hit and run tactics and each time it appeared that this program was being improved. It might be that the groups learning to fight like this also read history and learned from past mistakes. George was very interested with this type warfare. He began receiving battle information from the U S advisors stationed over there. These reports had him totally fascinated. George began injecting some actions from these battles for the students to check into and maybe to learn from. He was convinced that such warfare would be seen in future battles also.

George had researched and found some hidden battle tactics used by the French while they were involved in Vietnam. There were many classic battle plans used by the French against the jungle style hit and run tactics of the Vietnamese fighters. It seemed that most acceptable methods of warfare that the general world used in this time was being totally overcome by simple hit and run tactics in this jungle setting. Western fighting and thinking methods were totally off base from the normal Oriental thinking from individuals that were being trained by strong communist cadre. The cold war was also raging at this time. The republic thinking of the US was being matched against the communistic thoughts of Russia and China. These were very dangerous times for the entire world. George wove some strong procedures that the

US had used against the communist governments. No combat battles were being fought here, just open air blocking of various programs and plans being made by the other side. This began the dangerous game of who could build the biggest nuclear weapon. Threats against possible future actions were detailed through speeches, programs and planning. George was starting to interface actions, which included cold war tactics with hit and run ones. This he was finding would present some strong possibilities for future activities to be used by both sides in current foreign relations.

The modern Army was growing toward high technology used in weapons and equipment. George found he was struggling to keep up with all this modern material progression. He read everything new that came into the War College Library and talked with supply units that had been receiving the actual equipment. George could see that in the future, an enlisted man would probably need a college degree just to understand these new procedures. George now thought of a good thing. If he could get with any soldier who had come back from Vietnam and was stationed on the post, he could probably gain some very useful information. He went to the personnel office on post and talked with the people here. They in fact did have two men that had just returned from this country. They gave George the names

CHAPTER NINETEEN

and company they were assigned to. George wasted no time and drove right to the company. Here he met with the First Sergeant and talked with him for a time. The First Sergeant agreed that George could learn quite a bit from these men. He called them into the orderly room and introduced them to George. Even these men had heard of George. They would be happy to spend some time with George. The First Sergeant would allow the men a week off from here if they wanted to go with George and teach him what they had learned over there.

George drove back to his office bringing the two soldiers with him. They sat in his office and began talking with him about their knowledge of the tactics being used in Vietnam. George had no classes this day and this was considered working for him anyway. The men drove over to the club for lunch. They ate and sat around drinking a couple of beers. All this time, George was recording the information in his mind. He asked a lot of questions of the men and he was surprised that the way he had been thinking was filling right into the current practices of the military over there. The men agreed that everyone was just sliding their feet over there right now. The communist forces, the Viet Cong were much better trained for this type of war and the opposition had no idea what they were doing. The corruption within the government in the south was so bad that over 90% of the aid they were receiving was being grabbed by government officers. There was no control on this money after the southern government received it. This corruption continued on down the line and into the army ranks in the districts. The troops serving in the southern army had no desire to really fight. They generally were only there to draw money as they could. The opposition was very strong in their commitment to defeat the south. The US advisors here could not control any part of the army and were only along to support the troops or give advice if they were asked something.

The information that George had been getting was directly inline with this news. There would be no victory with the south if this system there continued. This was much worse than the Korean War had been. And the real fact of it being assistance to the southern army was keyed off political controls, not military. Civilians usually thought they could perform anyway they wanted to during a war and gain profits in the meantime. George asked the men to draw some battle plans out for him if they would. He needed original plans and the ending results. This he could teach with a historically correct background. These men he was teaching

CHAPTER NINETEEN

now would probably be involved over in Vietnam or some similar spots around the world.

The two soldiers spent the week with George and had begun to enjoy this work. George asked his boss if he could see about keeping these men for at least three months. He could use them in his classes as actual soldiers educated into the ways of Vietnam's tactics. The boss told George to see what he could get from the men's company. So they traveled to their company. George talked to the First Sergeant and then they both went to talk with the commander. This officer had graduated from the War College and knew about George. He figured if George could use the two men, they were all his as long as needed. He would have to carry them with this company however, for support backing. So this was great. George managed to get a couple of smaller desks to put near his office and put the two men to work. The two men started to work and they began pumping out lesson plans that were fantastic. Here was some reality information that might bring enlightenment to future personnel.

George next began bringing the men into his classes by giving the lesson and then called on the two to answer questions and to add more into the class regarding what might be met in future wars. George's program increased its enhancement to the students many times. The students were really getting into these lessons. Most had never seen such a class even at West Point. The two men stayed with the war College for over a year. They were then on new orders to return to Vietnam as they were very knowledgeable about this type of warfare. George hatred to see them go, but men like these were being begged for. One person with knowledge could assist a battalion sized unit to plan and conduct more solid battle plans. The cold war had been warming up more. The infamous Cuban crises was within a hair of dragging the US and Russia into a full war with nuclear weapons possible. The world was increasing in hot spot wars and many small war scenes, which George's lessons covered. There was no need to change lesson plans yet as everything being taught was in the same frame as before. It really did look as if all future wars would be following the battle plans from Vietnam and later such wars. Korea was just starting into battle plans involving hit and run tactic before the whole thing was called in a tie.

George and Fran had been talking about the world of dispute. George did not know when he might get called into such activity. He would be an asset to any unit due to his knowledge and massive study he gave this new war method. George did think that where ever he might get assigned he would be in the rear areas with his rank and knowledge. This

CHAPTER NINETEEN

was, as he believed anyway. Going overseas might assure him the next step promotion to Sergeant Major. The kids were grown enough to not require so much constant watching. They decided to just wait everything out and see how things went. George Jr. could help with yard work and mowing the grass. And Tracy would be able to help her mother.

George continued working at the War College and was still making officer friends. This generally was not tolerated within Army rules, but this was not a brazen disregard for rules. Past students still were dropping notes to George from where they were serving. Many times, they would pass very good information back regarding his lessons and their use in actual warfare around the world. This was a nice thing that George loved to hear.

A CROWN OF GLORY

CHAPTER TWENTY

A few more years were gaining on old age. George now was seeing his twenty years coming up before too much longer. He and Fran had talked, but neither really had any reason to think about getting out for a few years. George had become very involved with the War College and loved his work there. In a couple of years, George Jr. would be in high school and they would be able to watch his sports activities. Time marched on and the War College continued to run. Fort Leavenworth was at a full level for troops. George had been totally lulled into a relaxed state of almost retirement. His career was similar to a teacher in any school. George and Fran had made many friends here in the area and on the post. They were relaxed and skipping through life like kids do.

George came to work one day and found a note on his desk to see the Commander of the War College. He went right to his office and the secretary buzzed the General on the phone. She spoke for a minute with him and he came out to greet George. The General asked George to come in. He closed the door for some more privacy. He had a very serious look in his eye. They discussed the college here some and then he went to the main purpose. George was on alert for transfer for duty in Vietnam. This he had looked at and never believed he would get such an assignment. He would get a port call in three to five weeks. So he could begin getting things in order. He was remembering his alert for Korea so many years ago. The General told him he would get what leave he wanted. George thanked him and told the General he would see what he needed to do before leaving and this would guide him for the amount of leave he needed. The General agreed and released George for the day. George made a stop at personnel and got a list of what he needed to do before leaving. Next he drove home.

Fran saw him pull up to the house and had a question to what was going on. He must have forgot something here he needed. George came in the house and she could see

CHAPTER TWENTY

immediately that he had forgot nothing. She read his face and it was marked all over with the transfer information. She asked the question without making a sound. He told her he was on alert for Vietnam. They had discussed this so it really wasn't a bad shock. George told her about the leave and he had this list of what he needed to do prior to leaving here. He had some thoughts about staying at the War College until just before leaving. He could teach his class anyway until he left. He could get all the regular days off so this wouldn't be so bad. These tours in Vietnam were only a year in length, so it wouldn't be as bad as Korea was anyway. George would get a comfortable job in a rear unit and sit his days out. George did think he could learn more about his tactic knowledge in this more modern world. He was looking at this new assignment as a great new tool for him to grab and be able to use upon his return. Fran came over to George and held him again, just like she used to do. They had been stationed here a long time and George would probably be reassigned back here upon his return. So the two made their peace with the transfer. She next called her parents and advised them of the new information. Her mother knew this was a big shock to both of them. But in reality, George, like Ted, knew they were in the military to serve wherever they were sent to work. This was as it had always been in the world over for soldiers.

George called Bob and then Bill and told them. He asked if they wanted to come along. It might be like old times if they did. They both were very negative about this. George had no idea what they could be thinking of. Well the cast was set now and in the morning, George would report to the General. He would work two days a week to cover his classes until he left. The class would be almost up to graduation by this time. Maybe he could give just enough more information for these new officers to help a unit survive a rough time somewhere in the world. This night George and Fran sat together and told the kids about the news. George Jr. thought this was really neat. His dad would become another war hero in this war. Man he would have some stories to tell the guys at school. Tracy wasn't as happy as her brother however. She would miss dad while he was gone. The family spent the rest of the evening sitting and talked while watching some television.

The next morning, George headed back to the post. He went directly to the General's Office when he arrived. The secretary let him in as soon as he arrived. George told the General that he would finish his classes and work at least two days a week if this was ok. The General smiled and

CHAPTER TWENTY

thanked George. Actually he had felt that George would do something like this. The General told George that he would return here as soon as he came back. He couldn't afford to loose a man like him to another assignment. The days began running by now and George was taking care of things he needed to do before leaving. He was doing all this in his off days from teaching his class. The days were running hard now and the port call date was cruising in. George finally had everything done for the transfer and he took the last week off at home. He could sit here with Fran and just relax. He had given Fran power of attorney again and made sure everything else was up to date and in order. His start from here was to fly to San Francisco where he would catch a flight from Travis Air Base for Vietnam. Fran and the kids drove George to Kansas City to catch his flight there. He bid everyone goodbye and kissed the girls. He promised to write as soon as he was assigned over there.

George's flight took off and flew to Travis where he had an overnight wait for his flight leaving there. He was enjoying the good food and booze from the states. He was not sure if they would be on rations or what over there. The next morning, he was up, dressed and headed for the mess hall. This flight was to leave about 9 this morning. He ate a good breakfast, as the word was it would be sack lunches from now on. At nine, he boarded the plane and found a seat. A lot of his former students were on the flight, so he now was trapped. The officers finally drug him into the first class section where officers were seated. He suddenly was in class again. There were some officers here that hadn't went to the War College yet, so they got an advanced course in war tactics. The officers felt much better now that George was going over with them. They all swore to find him where ever his was assigned. It was a very long air ride to Vietnam. When the plane finally arrived there, the men were transported to assignment units. They would be transferred in a few days to their permanent duty station. The barracks where they were assigned for their stay here was hot, humid and very light. These buildings wouldn't stop a BB gun George was sure. The next morning, the men were taken to a huge room where they began getting their reassignments. When George stepped up, he was already assigned and had been expected. He was going to the 25th Infantry Division, headquartered in Cu Chi. There was a helicopter waiting to take him up there right now. He boarded the chopper and flew off to his new duty station. The flight was about 45 minutes and he was left at the helipad for the base. There were some men waiting for him and they introduced themselves and drove him to the orderly room. George

CHAPTER TWENTY

reported in and was met by quite a few men. The Commander here had been a student under George. Old times were flying now. So for tonight, George was released and told to report at 8 in the morning. He was advised the NCO Club was open on base and he might meet a few of his old buddies there. George walked over to the club and did meet a lot of men he knew. This 25th must be a center stage for meeting others here.

George was enjoying sitting and talking with other NCO's, whether he knew them or not. Almost all of them knew him. They all sat around and talked and discussed the mess over here. This was a fantastic play that presented everything that George had been teaching for years at the War College. George learned that the 25th was spread over three Provincial capitols. The main headquarters was here at Cu Chi. The group expected him to be assigned here, close to the head planning section. The senior men here were also telling George that it was not like Korea. There was no front line here. Cu Chi was getting mortared about two to three times a week. The sleeping quarters were not very secure. They were basically Quonset buildings with sand bags building a wall around the bottom. Inside, most of the beds had inside sandbags making walls. During a mortar attack, everyone jumped down to the floor and lay there until things were over. This way, many injuries could be saved even if a mortar shell landed in the center of the building. This place was not the luxury of stateside. But George laughed that it was better than a fox hole during the Korea War. Anyone that had been through that war agreed wholeheartedly. George sat and drank and was getting to feel fairly good. He finally was gone enough to make him think the bed would be a good place now. He headed to his barracks area and dropped into bed. He was told that he wouldn't be able to sleep through the morning noise and thus did not need a clock. George fell asleep and was gone to the world for now. About 2 in the morning, he was awoke and heard men yelling and mortars exploding. He did as he had been advised to and lay on the floor. The attack lasted only about 10 minutes. This was the normal span of time as the US could detect where the rounds were coming from and they would get return fire. They got it anyway in the general direction. The mortar crews here were ordered to fire in the general direction with hopes of getting something. After the attack settled down, people could be heard running around and checking on casualties. Seldom was there much damage that occurred but checks were made anyway. One of the NCO's in George's barracks told George to walk around in the morning to get an idea of what these attacks really did.

CHAPTER TWENTY

George awoke in the morning and just as he had been told, he needed no alarm. These places were noisier than barracks in the old days filled with green troops. George dressed, shaved and headed toward the mess hall. They had pretty good food compared to Korea. After he ate, he walked to the orderly room where he was listed as a member of this company. He reported in and was told to report to the headquarters of the division. He was being assigned there. So George found where this was and walked over to it. He was expected here as they already had a desk for him and a title. Once again, he became NCOIC of Operational Plans. So this might be interesting. He spent this day being introduced to all the men and officers around the headquarters. The Commanding General was a man known to George anyway. He had been a student some years back. He called George in and talked with him. This was so glad to have you with us talk, but a real happy thank god they sent you meeting. The General told George he would be the commander's right hand man from now own. All tactic information they had was being used and still the US forces were getting thumped hard. After the General completed talking with George, he was released to the operations officer for a briefing and daily report. This unit needed George and about 2 years ago.

A CROWN OF GLORY

George asked a favor. The operations officer told him to fire away. George wanted to walk the base and the perimeter area to get a good picture in his mind. The operations officer agreed by assigned three men to go with George. This was never a real secure area and he didn't want to lose George as soon as he had come here. And George definitely agreed with this. So now George and his bodyguard headed out. One of the men asked about a jeep. George told him no, he wanted to walk and think while viewing the area around. So the hike began. George walked through the camp first, looking at both sides. Next they began at the main gate and began walking around the perimeter. George would stop and write down some notes. He was thinking all the time and his body guard had no idea what he was seeing. All they saw was a perimeter wire with a clear fire zone around the camp. It was later in the afternoon before George and the body guards returned to headquarters. The operations Officer had no idea where they had been or when.

George now wanted a medium sized map of the camp. He was given this and sat down at his desk and began making marks and notes on the map. This was his beginning work sheet for his duties. George worked until late at night on his

CHAPTER TWENTY

map. The CQ was the only other person in the area. George
was glad to be involved once again in areas like this.

A CROWN OF GLORY

CHAPTER TWENTY ONE

The next morning George arose and did his morning routine. After breakfast he walked to the headquarters. He entered and sat down at his desk. Almost immediately, the Operations Officer came by and dropped a handful of reports in his in basket. George thanked him sarcastically and asked for a minute when he had time. Now was as good as any other. George showed him the map he had finished last night. He explained all the areas and the notes. The Operations Officer was flabbergasted and couldn't believe George could plat this map this well and so fast. Many of their problems with their perimeter were now showing. George recommended some fixes to help the current situation. The officer told him these would be fixed this day. Now everyone with any position in headquarters was called into a meeting. The last day's operations and other reports were discussed. Some people made recommendations, but George did not know these areas well enough as yet. He needed to check the maps he had in a section and do some studying. The General introduced George to the group and basically told them he was the same as the General right now. His reputation was without approach to military operations today. The meeting was dismissed and everyone gathered around George glad he was with the unit now.

George next asked the Operations Officer when he would be able to see the other areas assigned to the 25th Division. The Operations Officer told him probably tomorrow. This was a huge area to see and get around in. Transport was always by helicopter unless there was a field operation going on. The 25th Division was an armored division. George returned to his desk and got busy looking at maps and reading yesterday's operation reports. Slowly he was getting to know some of the areas that everyone was talking about. George began to work late since the only thing else to do was sleep and drink. He needed sleep and the drink would probably become a necessity later in a place like this. He still stopped by the club to talk with others for a short time. By six at night, basically only the CQ and George were around the headquarters. They of course had a duty officer, but very seldom did George ever see him.

George arose again in the morning and checked into the headquarters. Yesterday's reports were being distributed and George sat down and began reading his copies. Things looked a lot like a dart game at a carnival. The VC threw the darts and US balloons burst in a varied pattern. This was an old time turkey shoot where everyone brought their shotguns and spread lead balls all over the place and never hit much of anything that made a point. This did not really make very much sense. George knew the VC was out to win but they surely were heading in a round about way. The reports that George was reading were the same basic wording and forms that every thing he had seen here was. Just like in Korea, a new form of reporting had to be implemented. George wrote some notes up and gave them to the Operations Officer. George needed these changes in order to get good information. This requirement needed to be given to all under units that made reports. George needed good reports that he could read and understand what was really going on in the units out in the provincial areas. George might even need to go out and personally talk with the field units as he had in Korea. He decided he would attempt this change by writing instructions and sending such to the individual units. Then if this was missed by any, he could go out and personally train them. He talked to the Operations Officer once again and the man approved his plans. The Operations Officer had reserved a helicopter for George at 10 this morning. When the time came, George and an NCO from the operations section boarded the chopper and flew off. The NCO, Sam, was to answer questions that George might have while flying over the areas that the 25th Division was engaged in.

George landed at the major points of the 25th Division. In Tay Ninh City, they landed first. George talked with the Operations Section there and advised what he wanted now for the daily reports. They next flew to Dau Tieng and George talked to the Operations Section there. After this, the chopper flew around area where the division generally worked in. George was getting all new in sights into the landmass that the 25th was trying to cover. There were always firebases set out in areas and these generally were a good draw for night battles. By the end of the afternoon, George had a fairly good idea of the area the 25th covered. Now maybe he could look at the maps and get a mental picture of the real area. Upon their arrival back at Cu Chi, George went straight to his office and looked at maps. He studied them for about two hours and then walked to the

CHAPTER TWENTY ONE

NCO club. He had a few stiff drinks and then began to talk with some of the old in country people. He was trying to get a picture from the past and attach it to the present. Once this could be done, then he would have an idea what to look for in the future.

George finally went back to his barracks and crawled into his bed. He had a lot of thinking to do in the morning. This might be a good night to forget sleep. At 11, a mortar attack began. This was somewhat earlier than in the past. George and his barracks managed to get through this attack in good shape. The attack ended in about ten minutes, the usual for such attacks. George headed back to slumber land. At 1:10, the attack began again and this time lasted about 20 minutes. This was a new change for the attack times. George had been wondering if the pattern might change around here. There had been a lot of new changes to the US sweeps in the area. George felt doing the same thing was not helping the effort a bit. So the US changed, and now the VC was changing. Finally everyone got back into bed and George was wondering what would go next. At 3:30, the third mortar attack started. This time, a few rounds came in and they stopped. A coordinated attack to the front gate now began. The gate position was rapidly re enforced with standby troops. The attack cleared out about 15 minutes after it had began. Now the mortar rounds began falling again, continuing for about 20 minutes. By this time, everyone in camp had been up and down so many times this night that most just got dressed and walked outside to sit and listen for more incoming rounds. George walked to his office and dug his maps out. As he sat here studying the maps, he had something working in his mind and could not bring it out yet. He sat looking at the camp map that he had added things to just after he arrived here. He knew he was missing something here. The change in tactics by the VC was not made for fun and he was sure of this. He just couldn't put a finger on what it was.

This morning another meeting was called of the various operations groups. The General had added the Intelligence sections in to this also. Everyone sat around the large room and threw thoughts out for everyone to think about. Most of the section heads had written last night off as a very unusual operation but meaningless. The VC did change things every now and then, trying to confuse the US camps. George could agree with this, however he still was thinking there was a reason for the coordination of these attacks during last night's scenario. The word was in now that the attack on the main gate was a legitimate try as the men retrieved were VC sappers. These men were similar to the engineer forces that carried and placed explosive material. They had a reason for trying to get somewhere on the camp. Last night also had a different mortar arrangement for each attack. Each of the attacks was aimed at a small area in the camp. Generally before, they would set up and fire a few rounds all over the camp and quit.

After the meeting, George went back to his maps. He put the camp map on his desk and marked each area hit by mortars with different items. Next he put a rock at the main gate. As he sat looking at the map, he could almost see a picture here. The three mortar attacks formed an arrow point. This pointed to a section that George had marked on his map from his original look at the perimeter fence. The main gate attack still was odd. George now decided to drive out to the perimeter where the arrow point was going and also to check at the main gate. George signed a jeep out and grabbed two soldiers. He drove to the three areas hit last night. The mortar rounds had landed almost as if they had been placed right where they had hit. George looked about the perimeter area. He still had a concern about this section. He looked around the main gate and found nothing of any real interest. This had been a genuine sapper attack, as the VC did not waste valuable explosives. But they must have known they would have little chance of getting to the actual gate area. The response team was to backup the gate guards under just these types of attacks. George stopped right here. He had almost spoke what the purpose was, but just couldn't get to the true picture yet. George drove back to his office.

George sat at his desk and stared at his map. He could see some sort of plan the VC were planning or even practicing. The main gate attack was so strong yet. If they wanted the backup troops, then the attack had to be strong enough for their response. Suddenly a brick hit George on the head! He had it he was sure. He did some checking and found the information as to how he was thinking. Ok, George went to the Operations Officers office and asked to see him in the conference room. Here George lay the whole scene out. The point of the arrow in this last attack was the building where the main gate response team waited. The other parts of the arrow were buildings that were occupied on duty 24 hours a day. These places had men sitting outside in chairs most of the time. If you wanted to cross the perimeter wire at the place George had a feeling about before, you would need these building out of the play and the back up force over at the main gate. A person could move 100 or more troops into the camp from the perimeter and there was a chance that the main gate might be taken also. So this was the plan the VC had. The blocks in their way had now been removed and an

CHAPTER TWENTY ONE

attack could be expected during a night shortly after today. The Operations Officer left the room and got the General back to the room to see this. Once George explained the attacks, and then it was clear as a ten pound trout in a bathtub. Now the operations had to plan some sort of guarding group to oversee this area without being seen during the daytime. The General wanted at least one company spread around the perimeter area believed to be the of encroachment. These men would amble into their positions just after dark. They would have the night vision equipment and radios and phone back to their command.

The troops were set in and they waited into the night. About 1:30, the command received a call, telling them there was movement in the area just off the perimeter wire. Command advised the troops to stand by, as the VC probably would send in a small squad to check for troops. They probably wouldn't come very far in and then move back. The troops watched this happening. Shortly, there were herds of VC coming toward the perimeter. The company let things continue and made ready. The main gate began a fire fight now and the VC by the arrow was coming in strong. The troops at the end of the setting by the perimeter, waited until the VC had passed them and settled down to eliminate retreat by the VC. Now the mortar flares were fired and the

VC were caught in a slaughter plain. The battle took longer at the main gate. Within 15 minutes, the troops by the arrow were checking bodies for any wounded and not killed. These were taken to medical aid and would be held as prisoners of war.

The next morning came around and when George walked to his office, everyone in the area greeted him. The Operations Officer and the General were waiting for him in the Operations building. The General shook Georges hand and he thought his hand and arm was gone. This had been a great defeat for the VC. And there had been no movement that could be observed by enemy that might be watching. The body count from the plain had exceeded 200 so this was a major defeat for them. The General set up a party at the Officer's Club in the camp for this afternoon and evening. This plan had been pure genius and it was right in front of everyone. George had been the one to see it and plan against it. George was still building his fame.

CHAPTER TWENTY TWO

The days were running by rapidly since there were all kinds of work projects going now. George had set a special section up just to read and study events around the operations area of the 25th Division. George had started working close with the Division Intelligence staff. Between the two main sections, there was some invaluable information gathering. This section began decoding and identifying enemy plans still in the works. This was good as sometimes the VC didn't know what they would be doing and the 25th Division did. The section compiled reports within each command area and also gathered information covering the entire operations area. Word had began coming in that POW's were telling top brass that their commanders could not figure out what was happening. At times, before a plan was finished, the 25th Division had blocked the implementation of such plans. The VC commanders were looking hard for a spy amongst them. This was very funny to the 25th command personnel. Units all over Vietnam were requesting George to help them. Unfortunately George was only one man. If these units would send a man over to him, George would try to train the man somewhat along lines he operated under.

George was watching new things being reported now. There were rumors of tanks and heavy trucks coming down the Ho Chi Minh trail and entering into VC controlled areas. One such area was the Boi Loi woods, which was only a few miles from Dau Tieng. Arial observation was seeing a lot of new bunkers and such opening up in these woods. George created a second 'Iron triangle'. This would cover one side between Tay Ninh city and Dau Tieng. Another line was from Tay Ninh City to Cu Chi. Now the last leg was from Cu Chi to Dau Tieng and it ran right through the Boi Loi woods. George laughed and called this his steel triangle. It was interesting however to see what was beginning to happen in this area. The infamous 'Iron Triangle' also included the Boi Loi woods. In addition to the heavy equipment reports, there was information coming about NVA troops in large numbers

CHAPTER TWENTY TWO

coming down the trail. One report listed that 3 NVA Division were set up in the Boi Loi woods. George could not imagine what a large group of troops would be planning. They didn't need that many to wipe the 25th Division's camps out. The 25th began running some operations around the areas and were getting only light contact with the enemy. These new troops either were not there or they were very well trained. Each new intelligence photo of the areas were showing movements and changes in areas around the Boi Loi woods. Most of the changes were very small ones and had to be looked at carefully. There was plenty of cover in the woods. George tried to get an operation set up in these woods, but no one would do such in case there were a large force in there. They would never get them out in time.

So George and his section continued to read reports and plot information on their big wall map. George went to the Division information library and looked through it. He needed some old information about this country. There was a history book at the library and this might help George. George asked if he could take this book to his quarters. He was given the book and George took if to his office first. He sat at his desk and began reading the book. The history of this country was fascinating and was showing that there had been very little peace here. Most of the fighting had been with each other or different oriental people. George was reading some very interesting things. One mutual area that was shared by most oriental peoples was their celebration of their new year. This was called Tet and was almost a holy day for them. Many things had occurred during this period of time. The Tet holiday lasted some times up to two and three weeks. In the oriental mind, how things went over Tet, would show what the rest of the year would be like. This was very interesting to George. He was seeing that the oriental mind worked totally different in some areas than a western mind. George pulled some old reports out and looked through them again. He was getting on the brink of a new discovery he thought. Something was hatching inside his little brain.

George moved from the maps to reports, and then back to the book. This whole routine was working out a new vision for him. Something that was really bothering him was the fact that during times when the Vietnamese people were fighting, some of their largest battles were set up during the Tet holiday. Once again, how the holiday went, so would the year go. Tet was only about two months away now. If this history repeated itself as most of it does, then the coming Tet could be scheduled for something. The more recent reports were showing a large build up, especially in the Boi Loi

CHAPTER TWENTY TWO

woods. George needed more intelligence on this, so he went to the S-2's Office. Here, the CO introduced him to his main man and he was considered an expert on oriental operations. George and him sat and talked for a long time. The man seemed to know what he was talking about. The two studied recent reports on a possible build up of men and equipment. George asked about the possibility of an offensive over the Tet holiday. The intelligence man shook his head. He said generally such things had to cooperate with what the year was. In other words, strong offensives would more likely come during a year of the bull, or a year of the dragon. This coming year was the year of the monkey. So George thanked him and went back to this office. He read up on the year of the monkey in his history book.

A year of the monkey could mean a lot of things. The monkey is considered a fast, small creature that works with his own tribe. They can battle much larger animals by all sticking together. Monkeys can also hide in treed areas. George read a lot of information about the monkey. He gathered as much information as he could and then tried to set this information into a military mode. He was surprised about how versatile the monkey really is. This now blew the Intelligence NCO's information out. He probably had never dug into information about this before. George now got into gear, placing various situations for the VC against various targets. He could not see why so much equipment and manpower was showing up in the Boi Loi woods. They would need far less to attack any of the main units around this region. George sat and looked at the map and even daydreamed some. In fact he was getting sleepy just doing this. He almost needed a nap. But his brain was running on full throttle as yet, even though he was sleepy. George now walked outside and moved around for a while. He needed the fresh air the think better. He walked about for almost a hour and then went back inside. He returned to his desk and sat down. He looked at his map and then it seemed to move. It turned just right to be in line with the real territory outside. Suddenly George saw the whole picture. He jumped up and yelled. The Operations officer came almost on the run. George pointed to the map and began reading the details out loud to everyone. The Boi Loi woods was an excellent staging area for a coordinated attack on small local units and on Saigon itself. With the masses that were being reported and the equipment, they just might be able to overtake the city if no one was expecting it. If Saigon fell, basically the rest of the country would go down also. This was in front of everyone all along, but no one could see it. George didn't see it right away either.

CHAPTER TWENTY TWO

The Operations Officer called up to the General's Office and asked if he could come over. He agreed and walked to the Operations Office. Once inside, he was shown George's map of the area. As the General stood there and looked, he got the information and you could tell it on his face. He was almost ashamed as he was a graduate from the War College and had studied under George. He should have seen this right off the bat. George told him not to be concerned. George had all the reports and information and had only now seen things clearly. The General now needed to get into Saigon and talk with the command there. Tight security was now placed on this. No one wanted this information to get out and have the enemy find out the southern section already knew what was to happen. Now the division needed as much new reports as they could get. New plans had to be made to help fortify their camps.

The 25th at Cu Chi was figuring things out very well and they would be ready for what ever might come. When the General returned from Saigon, he called George into his office. He asked if George would mind going to Saigon and meeting with the top brass there. They needed to find out exactly how George figured this operation out. And as a second award, they wanted to send George to Hawaii to meet his wife there. They would fly her to Hawaii and they could

A CROWN OF GLORY

R&R for a week. This sounded fantastic to George. He and Fran had discussed this, but he wasn't sure if he could get the approval. Now they were the approval. So George packed some clothes and operations called for a helicopter to take him there. He headed out the next day. They had programmed two days in Saigon before he would leave for Hawaii. He arrived and sat down with all the top military leaders and set the map up just as he had at Cu Chi. Immediately the officers saw the plan also. Just a simple movement of the map and everything jumped off the paper and into human minds. George explained to them about the research he had done also. He told them of the book title and that it was in the 25th official library. They should have a copy around here somewhere. The big shots thanked George and asked him if he would mind sitting down with their NCO personnel and explaining the system to them. If they could grasp the methods used by George, then maybe they could find things in the future like he had. George had to wait until his flight to Hawaii anyway, so he was willing to meet with the men.

George spent a day and some with the men and tried to spread a crash course for them. He gave them some plan problems and asked them to find an answer by the time he came back from Hawaii. They dove into the planning with a strong will to find out what was going on. When the appointed time came for George to catch a ride to Hawaii, he was checked in and got aboard the plane. He would now have some time to ride again. This would be some shorter than the first trip over to Vietnam. George had brought a book to read and he also slept some. Finally the plane began its descent to land in Hawaii. George walked into the terminal and retrieved his suitcase. He walked back into a meeting area between family and soldiers. Fran was there waiting for him. She had already obtained a hotel room, and had been just sitting here waiting for George. They went to the visitor information room and got some pamphlets about how and what to see here. They sat down and began planning some things they might be interested in. They decided to just relax for this day and start in the morning. They went to their room and rested. George even got a small nap. Just about dinner time, they decided to try the hotel restaurant. It was surprisingly good and not bad in price. After this they walked around in the cool evening. This was real luxury since no one could walk around town in the evening over in country. They had chosen some things to do tomorrow and they didn't need reservations. The military command here was set up to assist soldiers on R&R. They reserved so many seats or places on everything about tourism. This way a first come, first served system was working. George and Fran had a lot of fun on this vacation. They were building memories that they would carry the rest of their lives. The week passed to rapidly and soon it was time to say goodbye. George's plane left about a hour before Fran did. They had finished their stay and it had been wonderful. George told Fran goodbye and he would see her soon. He only had about four months left.

CHAPTER TWENTY THREE

When George arrived back in Saigon, he went to the headquarters building and checked on his 'students' here. They gave him their answers and were very close to being correct. George explained to everyone that all a person really needed was good current information and an ability to question and figure things out. He went to the offices of the top leaders and thanked them for the R&R. He told them when ever they needed anything, just call. If he could help them, he would. He now went to the in country transport desk. He asked about a flight to Cu Chi. The desk clerk here told him they had one and as soon as the VIP showed up, they could leave. George gave his name so they could call him. The clerk looked at his name and gulped. He was the VIP. So ok, the helicopter was up and away. He would really have to work to get used to being here again. Especially after the vacation in Hawaii. George arrived and walked into the Operations office. Everyone was glad to see him back. And he had a lot of work in his in basket. This was exciting, right? George just checked in and walked to his barracks. He lay down on his bunk and caught a nap. All the running he was doing, was really bringing him a tired body. He finally got up to go get some supper at the mess. He walked over to the day room and see if anyone was around there. Nothing exciting there, so he walked to the club. Here he knew a lot of the guys. They talked and ribbed George about his R&R. And he told them he really had not wanted to return. Well he would be finished here before very much longer.

Tet holiday was just around the corner now. George was looking over the plans that had been made. They all looked fairly good except the one operation very close to the Boi Loi woods. George did not like this as it could set some questioning off among the VC commanders. George went to talk with the Operations Officer. George told him about his thoughts. The officer did agree, but told him the General had requested this operation. This was one of those things that managed to trip up many good operations. You could do nothing about this. George looked over other plans that various units had made for their readiness for the coming Tet. George told the Operations Officer about their plans for around Saigon. Things appeared to be almost geared up for whatever might be engaged. Other military units were not accepting George's information about the coming offensive. This was going to hurt many people. The navy and marines did not accept George's layout of what the VC and others were planning to do. George felt sorry for them, as their positions would be hard hit and possibly overrun. This was sort of like the old saying –'You can lead a horse to water but you can't make him drink'.

The Operations section continued to monitor all the intelligence and operational plans. All messages transmitted around the 25th area was also monitored with the hopes that others would soon wake up. But they were not doing very well along this line. All George and his section could do was wait and hope. There was beginning to get more enemy contact for various units around. When Tet finally arrived, the balloon went up. Suddenly the whole southern part of the country was under massive attack. Many units were taking an horrible beating and they were losing because they had not been prepared. The enemy had planned this operation out fully. They knew the systems they were using and were matching very much ahead of their stated targets. The equipment that the enemy now had was amazing to US military units. This was the real show of what the North Vietnamese Army had available to use. Their equipment mixed with their hit and run tactics was proving devastating to the US forces.

George began requesting large patrols in directions out from the camps. These patrols could show if there was any movement around the camps, and this might assist the camps to reinforce particular sections of their perimeter fence lines. Extra claymore mines were placed all around and there were now guard posts about every 200 yards. Each of these had phone lines back to the command center. Every third guard position had a starlight scope also to enable them to see in the dark better. There were back up force units behind the perimeter and half the men on at all times. The camp was on a 12 on, 12 off duty system. Of course many sections like George's were mostly on. There were no large scale attacks to any 25th location as yet. Saigon was getting pounded as well as some other provincial headquarters. Everyone continued to maintain a status of high alert. There was no guarantee that everyone would be hit or not hit. The best thing was to stay ready for whatever might come around.

Reports continued to come in daily and the Operations section could plot the battles as they continued. Still there was not much from the 25th Division camps. Reports also came in about entire positions of more than a regiment were being overran and driven out. These camps were generally those of the marines or navy. They would listen the next time someone told them what was coming. The first month was passing from the Tet offensive. More and more smaller camps were now being attacked and such losses were very bad. Cu Chi had began to close down some of their 100% readiness troops and ease life for the servicemen stationed at 25th camps. A firm watch was still maintained at all facilities, but not in so large a number. Things around the country were finally beginning to edge back down to a more peaceful time. George was keeping track of his reports as yet and was seeing the slow down as an event planned to pull hard line NVA troops back for future service. Reports were again showing up to three NVA Divisions back in the Boi Loi woods. There was a slow down toward neutralization of the large enemy NVA troops.

George and his section had not shut down very much as yet. Everyone had seen what could arise in a very short time, so they continued monitoring reports, transmissions, and operations around their areas. A small district headquarters bordering on the Boi Loi woods was base for a small group of six American advisors and about 2 companies of PF Vietnamese troops. They also had a battery of ARVN 155 guns. Into March, this small place was hit very hard and was all but over ran with everything being used in support of them, including Spookies and Light Fire Teams. Cu Chi headquarters decided to sent out a relief column in the morning to assist these troops. The armored convoy departed about 6:30 from Cu Chi and headed toward the district headquarters. About 10 Kilometers off the camp, this column ran into an ambush. There were 40 armored vehicles put out of action in seconds. This was a terrible blow to all involved. This ended up being one of the worst operations for the 25th. It evidently had been planned for this very action. The VC expected Cu Chi to send out a relief for the little district headquarters. The 25th Division lost over 150 dead over this ambush. When this ambush was over, everything stopped all around. There was little movement or action seen any where close to this area.

The Operations section now began to notice that all hard activity had stopped and no new action had been seen. Very small groups of hit and miss operations. The 25th Division could run major operations once again and find no major problems. George had not been deceived into believing that the VC were closing down. This probably was just a hold over from the major offensive they had just ended.

CHAPTER TWENTY THREE

George advised all their units to continue a good watch and keep their reports continuing in. He wanted everything that they heard, saw, and even felt. He had schooled all units in how to report things forward, not leaving anything out thinking it was ridicules. George also took another walk around the perimeter of the Cu Chi camp. He looked every inch of the ground over and saw nothing new or unusual. He talked with all patrol members every time they went out. There really wasn't much moving now. George would sit for hours looking at maps. He was beginning to think that something new was being planned now. Generally a major offense would taper off, but usually the local contacts continued. It almost seemed that the enemy was attempting to make the US forces think they had given up.

George was back now at the camp club. He listened and talked to everyone and anyone. He was not learning much here either. George figured if he wasn't getting much information from the club, then he would come around anyway and have a few drinks. He enjoyed sitting in the club and listening to idle chat without any care about what else might be happening around here this night. George used this as a getaway from his office problems. Like the old saying, - 'Too much work and not enough play', George needed his off time now. This had been happening more as he learned to enjoy off time more. George had made a lot of friends here also. He was becoming a fixture of just sitting and listening and talking with some friends. He really didn't care much for playing cards, and other such things that were available. George had finally gone over his twenty year mark and he could retire whenever he wished. At this time George still wanted to hang on for awhile. Once he got back to the world, then his military job would probably be back to teaching. George enjoyed his work at the War College. He had been learning many things over here also. He did think that once back in the states, he would retire if he got orders to come over here. From what he had seen at this point this thing might still continue for years. This was covered by the book he had read about the constant state of war within this region. The sad thing was the casualties left from this never ending plight of the people. The poor Vietnamese farmers worked seven days a week in their fields, and paid tax to the south government and to the VC. He was lucky to have enough to feed his family after all this. The main help the US was giving them was some jobs that paid very well, compared to their local standards. Maybe someday there would be justice for all this.

George told everyone good night and walked back to his barracks. He was tired anyway and the drinks had

CHAPTER TWENTY THREE

improved this condition. Most people did not have to worry about insomnia around here. George had talked with some long range patrol soldiers and they told him you did not dare sleep very sound out in the bush. A person had to gage every action to make sure you didn't do something that might point you out to enemy. George was too old to go on duties like the patrol units. He had done similar things when he was younger and now he was allowed to just watch others. One of the perks for old soldiers was a gift of not having to work this hard. George checked his uniform for tomorrow and was satisfied, so he climbed into bed.

A CROWN OF GLORY

CHAPTER TWENTY FOUR

The early morning came around hard as by 4:30 mortar rounds were falling again on the camp. George figured the local VC had finally stepped back into their previous procedures. This incoming of rounds now was back like it was before the Tet offensive. George figured he might as well stay up now since it was late enough to wait for duty time. George went outside and felt the cooler air and sat down there. He sat for about an hour and finally went back inside and put his uniform on for duty. He walked over to the mess hall after cleaning up and had breakfast. There was some talk this morning about the night's entertainment. George smiled to himself. He walked over to his office and went through his in basket. He was getting reports already about this attack last night. The men on duty had directed the location of the mortar tubes to the northeast. They gave a co ordinance and George looked on his map on the wall. This was a new location that hadn't been used before. George was thinking maybe the other side was cranking up again. This would be more proven if there were more attacks during this week.

The Operations Officer came into the building just after George. They greeted each other and the officer asked George what he thought about last night. He really didn't have a solid answer right now, but off hand he would say they were getting back into their pre-Tet operations. They also had fired from a new location never used before. Now they would have to sit and wait for more reports. George wanted a patrol put out in the direction of this attack. Maybe they could find something new to help out. George had already traced the direction and probable firing location. The rounds sounded like 61 mortars, which did not have the range of the larger units. These however were much easier to carry and hold for firing. George would have to look hard at anything a patrol might find. He also needed to pay very close attention to all reports coming in this day. This day promised to be an action based one. George needed to run around to other sections on base and find what they were getting in from their commands under them. This would take up to a week to get everything in from the outer units. The Operations section would have a full day now and they needed to pay very close attention.

George sat back down at his desk and re read all the morning's reports. He really didn't think he would find anything more out. The section would now have to wait until more information was obtained and transmitted to them. George had an idea and drove out to the perimeter wire where the last attack was ran. He sat here looking outside and thinking. He must have sat for about an hour when a guard patrol pulled up. The sergeant driving told George this was not a secure area and he really shouldn't be here. George agreed but told the guard who he was and what he was looking for. George couldn't see or think of anything so he drove back. He had been back in the office about 10 minutes when a mortar attack began during the daytime. Now this was really unusual and he had no idea what this might lead to. The Operations Officer called for a conference with all section heads to be held at 1 this afternoon in the conference room. At least everyone could sit here and look stupid instead in their offices. Intelligence had no idea why this attack had occurred during the daytime. The enemy must have been hoping that more bodies would be around during this time of the day. George ordered a helicopter for a scouting run and invited anyone who could use information to come along. Intelligence sent a man, and a man from the base operations came along also.

The flight was planned to pass around the areas off the base where previous night attacks had usually came from. No one could see anything new in these areas. Now George had an idea and asked the pilot to search on the opposite side of the camp. They reached this area and began to see working sign almost immediately. The enemy had swung around to this side, as there was not much air traffic here. They probably had been working this side since the last night mortar attack. Of course they might have been working here before that even. They may have set that attack up to draw the camps attention to that area. George could see what appeared like from the air as new bunker positions. There were some that were only about 2 kilometers from this perimeter of the camp. George made a note to schedule this area into the camps H & I firing during the nighttime.

The scouting trip ended and George walked to his office once again. He plotted on his wall map what the new area appeared like now. This area had never shown much activity. Other areas out from the camp had been showing a lot of movement but nothing close to the camp. George sat by

CHAPTER TWENTY FOUR

his desk and did some very deep thinking. There were too many missing pages to a correct scenario from what anyone had at this time. George asked for a daytime patrol to circle the camp out about a half-kilometer. This was now set for the next morning. George wanted the patrol to carry a small cartridge camera with them. He needed some pictures of what they might discover. There were just too many empty pages as yet, but something was going on. George walked out the building and headed toward the club. He entered and sat down next to a small table. He could generally hear most of the conversation going on here. George sat here and had a few drinks and he kept hearing talk that sounded like a couple of tunnel rats. He wanted to talk with these guys. He had always been interested in their dangerous duty. He found them and asked if he could sit with them. The two readily agreed to having him here. They knew who he was and they could tell him a lot of things that most soldiers had not idea about. The three men sat and drank, talking about tunnels and what you could find in some of them. A person never knew what might lay ahead for them. Generally, someone in this occupation over here did not have a long lifeline. Each time a person went down a tunnel hole, it might be his last. George asked the guys if these tunnel ever caved in. They really didn't know for sure, but there was always a good thing to watch for. They indicated the place next to the perimeter fence line on the west side. This was called a sinkhole by most but these men were sure it had been a tunnel.

George asked all sorts of questions about many items related to tunnels. He was genuinely interested in these things. He asked many questions and the guys told him as best they knew. At lest he was getting things from the horses mouth. These guys had told him about tunnels that had survived from when the French were over here. Many of these tunnels had been found below major cities. They almost never caved in unless they had been made fast and sloppy. Generally the tunnel had numerous exits and this helped during bombing raids. A B-52 bomber could bomb an area with tunnels and if a bomb hit on top of a tunnel, just that section was hurt. Finally George thanked the guys and walked back to the office. He sat at his desk for a few hours now, just thinking the tunnel information over. Finally he walked to his barracks and showered and went to bed. He had not been hungry after the exciting information he was getting and the drinks involved.

The next morning George got ready and walked to the office. He began going through the daily reports from around the different camps. He asked the sergeant that had

CHAPTER TWENTY FOUR

arranged the patrol for today if they might be back before noon. The sergeant told him they could be, but he would rather think about 2. So George walked over to the Division library once again and checked on present and past tunnel findings. He found a book, but it mostly covered such networks from the era that the French were here. He took this anyway and walked back to the office. He sat at his desk and began running through the pages. The French had many nightmares involved with tunnels. Many of their bases were dug under with tunnels housing sometimes more enemy than they had on top. George thought about the Bio Lio woods. handle a division of soldiers and not leave much sign on top. George sat at his desk and was almost studying this book. He ran right through lunch and didn't even think about eating, once again. An assistant finally got his attention and advised the patrol had returned. They were waiting for him in the conference room for his debriefing. He walked over there and met the men. He asked some questions and the sergeant in charge stood up walked by the chalkboard and began a outlay of the patrol. He told of their movement, their speed, and their various finding of interesting material and sign. He drew schematics and pictures on the board, explaining everything. They had taken pictures but the film wouldn't be back for 2 or 3 days. George now asked the Sergeant to outline all this on a wall map as he had done on the board. The rest of the men were busy agreeing and giving additional information they had seen. Finally when the debrief was finished, George had some of the information he had been waiting for. He walked to his office and charted the information on his wall map. He asked the Operations Officer for a meeting with all section heads in the morning in the conference room. He had some mind-blowing information to give out.

George walked back to the club to see if the tunnel rats would be there again. They weren't so George asked about them. He was told they should be here in about 10 minutes, according to their normal schedule. George sat down and waited. The men came in almost on time. George asked them to sit with him if they would. They agreed and George bought drinks around. He had a small bombshell for them, if they didn't already know. He told them about the patrol he had originally organized and about the rough results. The men were just sitting there and smiling. George stopped and asked them about their knowledge of these things. They had known since almost their arrival in country about the tunnels. They had tried to get the information to the right hands, but they only met disregard and file 13 for their efforts. George showed them the rough sketch of the

CHAPTER TWENTY FOUR

camp perimeter and it followed what he had known. George had just now began to suspect this monster. He had the ball now. He asked if the guys could be available in the morning for a conference with the section heads of the camp. They really weren't anxious but they would go if George wanted them to. Now the three just sat, drank, and talked about non-important things. This time however, George was getting hungry since he had missed supper last night and lunch today again. George finally said good night to the guys and walked to the mess hall.

After dinner, George walked over by the office and sat in a chair outside, enjoying the cooler evening air. A couple of other guys from the office came by and sat down with George. They generally were just passing time with talk. Nothing business wise was entered into. Some times it was just nice to sit and pretend you were sitting on your porch at home. The day's work over here was very wearing and a person could get very tired of every thing involved. The three guys were talking about the states now and some happy memories back home. George was down to about two months yet. He had been working very hard compared to his job at the War College. Finally the three were tired enough to head for their barracks and get some needed sleep.

A CROWN OF GLORY

CHAPTER TWENTY FIVE

When the morning came, George got up and made ready for the new day. He walked to the mess hall and ate breakfast. After this he walked to the Office thinking about the conference this morning. He checked the morning reports in his in basket and found what all had occurred over the night. After all this, he walked over to the conference center to make sure everything was ready for this meeting. He had set a wall map up of the camp and also a chalkboard. Soon section heads and their associates began arriving. Soon almost everyone was here and it was about time to start. George stood in the front and thanked everyone for coming. About this time, the General entered the room. He told everyone to be at ease and he sat down. George continued on. He had a suspicion that there might be problems under this camp. He talked about the many times he had walked the perimeter of the camp and watched everything outside. Small things and nothing big were changed. He had read the information in a book from the Divisions library and added this to the camps perimeter. Next he had talked with two very knowledgeable Tunnel Rats. And finally he had a patrol to walk the outside of the perimeter about a half a Kilometer out. He had their report also. He now brought the mess forward. There was currently a sizeable enemy force directly under this camp. George now had everyone's attention. He continued on with areas where trapdoors were found and bunker openings that were completely hidden. After his briefing he called the two tunnel rats up to give their knowledge about things under the camp. After all the information was out, the group had a question and answer session and a conference about what to do now.

What the group was thinking was getting written information on what each unit here could do to help with this problem. The EOD section would need to advise if they could blow trapdoors and keep things permanently closed or not. So this afternoon, Operations would send out the questionnaires and see what might pop up. These papers

CHAPTER TWENTY FIVE

needed to have a suspense date on them so return information could be gathered after only a short time. The tunnel rats could not answer if the underground forces might pop up inside the camp or not. The ability was here, but would this be too dangerous for them to enact. George and his crew would study the replies and select what the best programs would be able to combat this new threat. So now the Operations Officer closed the meeting and thanked everyone for their priority of getting information for this problem. Everyone left the building and walked back to their offices.

It was almost noon so many men were heading for the mess hall. George stopped by his office first to see if anything important had come in while he was at the meeting. His in basket was still empty so he headed for the mess hall. He was walking down the street and he thought he heard mortars being fired. He stopped for a minutes and he was sure they were being fired. Now he heard the incoming rounds. They were getting close and a round hit about a half block away. George began running for some protection. He felt some sharp pains in his back and legs, but heard nothing. He fell to the ground and looked ahead. He couldn't hear anything and saw a blurred sight ahead. A man ran up to George and checked him. George saw his face for a minute and then it slowly went black. The Operations Officer ran up to see how he was. He looked at George and the man checking him told him it was all over for George. He had passed fast however so didn't face much pain. The medics pulled up with their ambulance and George was put on a stretcher and taken to the hospital. A doctor checked him there and told them to take him to the coroner's section.

This loss was devastating to the operations section and in fact the entire Division. The General heard the news and did all but cry. He called the Operations Officer and told him to write George up for the Congressional Medal of Honor, and it would be awarded to George posthumously. George had always asked his superiors not to turn him in for this award as he felt he hadn't done anything special. The General declared a day of mourning for the entire Division. Now the word headed back to the states for his family and friends. The CMH was rushed through for getting it to his wife and family before very long after their services for him.

The 25th Division General contacted the War College General about the sad news. The General for the college advised the post he would notify the family. He gathered his aid and drove out to George's family and house. Fran was sitting in the living room of the house with her parents. She saw the military car drive up and wondered what or who this was. Then she saw the General and his aid. She suddenly

CHAPTER TWENTY FIVE

had a pit in her stomach as she walked to the front door. She opened the door and looked at the General and saw his eyes. She could not think, talk, or cry. She was completely void of any reaction, mental or physical. Her parents saw what was happening and Lucy began to cry. Ted got up and walked to his daughter and held her. Now she grabbed her dad and began sobbing. The General just stood for a minute and was quiet. Then he told Ted that anything they needed to let him know. George was getting the CMH award, and he would have information for them at a later date as to the circumstances. The General told Ted he would stop by in a few days to see if they needed anything yet.

The General left and Ted helped Fran over to the couch and set her next to her mother. He now sat with both of them and tried to show a presents near them. The whole family had just been devastated by the news. Ted felt very shocked and horribly vacant by this loss. The mother and daughter had nowhere to turn now except to him. George would have turned 40 in two months. The pain for Fran was not transferable to her mother or father. The children still had to find out about their father. Ted figured he needed to stay here for the night. There was no telling what Fran would feel like or even do. A situation like this tore families very hard. War is like that and still idiots in high offices continue to enter into war just to satisfy their own egos. Ted did call Bill and Bob and let them know. They were almost family and maybe they could help some with Fran and the kids. When the kids came home from school, Ted took them outside and told them the news. He sat with them for over an hour outside. He told them their mother was very upset and he did not want them to grieve yet with her. Everyone had always known this situation what could have happen. What George left to the world was much more than anyone else has left for hundreds of years. This they had to accept. George had left a legacy that was unequaled.

Finally the whole family got together and sat around the living room. Bill and Bob arrived with their wives and attempted to help as they could. Sandy and Ann had also been crying, as this was evident in their faces. Ted had wiped tears from his eyes also. The country had lost one of the best heroes they ever had. There was little talk going around now. It was more like a kind of wake with everyone grieving deep within themselves. Fran had a huge empty spot and felt numb all over. Word had gotten into town now and friends were bringing food dishes over for the family here. Ted had to assume charge for the family. He thanked everyone and made a note so he could return the dishes to the proper person. The minister came by and talked with everyone. He

CHAPTER TWENTY FIVE

really couldn't help very much but he stayed close in case there was something he could do. The day passed slowly and the hurt dug down into everyone's souls. It was impossible to look on George's life with thankfulness about his accomplishments. The only thing at this time was the whole torn into everyone who knew and loved him. Evening slowly crept in and Bill, Bob, and their wives took leave to go home. They had families to take care of there also. Tracy got things ready for this family for a supper or snack, whatever the family wanted. Fran was reduced into a shell and couldn't think or act. Her entire life had ended with a single message. The rest of the family could not help her. They stayed available to give any comfort they could, but she just huddled at the end of the couch and stared across the room. Finally the kids went to bed and Ted checked the bed in the spare bedroom. Lucy and him would stay here for the night at any rate. They did not attempt to move Fran at this time. She had no ability to think or move. Ted sat up with her for a large portion of the night. He didn't say anything, but he was there is she needed him.

The next day, Ted went to the local undertaker and had him begin plans for the funeral. The army had left a paper with Fran and Ted found it and read the information it had. George would arrive at Fort Leavenworth tomorrow.

A CROWN OF GLORY

The undertaker could retrieve the body and begin preparations for the funeral. Ted had to get the gravesite going. George and Fran had purchased burial plots many years ago. They also had made arrangements for their funerals and had this paid. Ted had things easier because of this. The undertaker told Ted the funeral should be held two days after the body arrived. He would take care of notifications in the local papers. He also had contacted the Army for their services at the post. They would hold this as George had been so well known on this post and many more. The funeral would be a closed casket one and Fran's local minister would officiate the service. Ted had finally finished all the preparations. Lucy had been staying with Fran and doing what she could. Fran had started moving around some on this second day. She still was folded up within herself. She was enclosed in a small room in her soul where she and George could share their personal love.

The day of the funeral arrived and Lucy helped Fran get dressed. The kids were doing good so far and this day would be a painful goodbye to George. The funeral service area of the undertakers was large, but it could never hold the amount of people who came to pay their regards to George. The crowd filled the outside lawn area and blocked off the street. This was just in the small town. The service later at

CHAPTER TWENTY FIVE

Fort Leavenworth was going to require a lot more space. Ted, Bill and Bob spoke at the service. They each gave some inside information about George and the bond they had with George through his life around here. George's military career had saved thousands of lives and instilled outstanding performance of the men with whom he served. A great loss was felt from George's leaving but his principles would continue forward in the service of his country. Hundred's of years into the future would find George's principles still working to save men.

The procession to the cemetery was very long and took a lot of time. At the cemetery the Army had an honor guard. He was given a 21-gun salute and taps were played over the horizon. After the ceremony at the cemetery, the men escorted Fran home. She was an empty wreck now with no hope of finishing her life with George. She did have their children yet so not all was lost. Lucy was a big help now for Fran. Her mother helped with the kids, made sure they ate good and had clean clothes. Fran was not much good for anything yet. She had years ahead now without her love and she wasn't sure if she could handle the rest of this day, let alone years ahead. Ted and Lucy were still having some problems them selves missing George, but they had to stay strong now for Fran and the kids. They both had their mourning times and tried to keep this to themselves. The kids were having difficulty also but their friends were helping them to see through these torn days.

CHAPTER TWENTY SIX

Weeks had now passed and Fran had finely accepted her loss, but she could not regain her old happiness and strength. The General from the War College had been coming around about once a week. A couple of times, he had brought his wife with him. Fran liked his wife and they were able to talk about things that she couldn't handle with anyone else. One afternoon, the General and his wife drove out to Fran's place. The kids had just came home from school. The General asked Fran and the kids to drive to the post with him, as he had something to show them. They got into his car and he headed for the post. As they approached the War College, they noticed that a large crowd was in front of the building. The General got out and led Fran and the children up to chairs in the front. Next he took the podium and began to talk. This gathering was for a tribute to a great man that the entire world looked up to. A large brass plaque was unveiled showing George's face and some wording about his life's work here. On top of the whole plaque and stand was a shiny brass helmet. 'The Crown of Glory' was written under the helmet.

This episode was now a small closure for Fran. This probably did more for her than anything else had up to date. Fran talked some on the way back to her home. She thanked the General for all he had done for her and the family. What Fran and the children now faced was a life of memories only of George. His presence would no longer be here. George had put aside his mortal 'Crown of Glory' and replaced it with the pure 'Crown of Glory'. When the family arrived at home, Ted and Lucy were there waiting for them. Ted had figured they were out with someone. Fran thanked everyone that she could in her mind and walked into the house. Her parents and kids came along also and everyone sat in the living room. Fran told her parents what had been done out at the post. They were amazed how well she had taken this and that she was finally talking again. This had been a beneficial

CHAPTER TWENTY SIX

ceremony and she had gained some acceptance of her loss at last. The kids were even doing better.

Fran now was basically back to a normal life without her love. She received papers from the army which told her about the CMH award and that George had been retired by the Army after over twenty years service. This gave Fran about 80 % of George's pay for the rest of her life. In addition she would maintain shopping rights on post. George also had a government insurance for policy for $20,000. He also had a couple of larger policies. Fran and the kids would be well looked after. Ted suggested they all go out to eat tonight. This would keep everyone from having to cook and clean up. Even Fran agreed to this. She asked if they could go to the post and eat at the club there. She knew she had to face this exposure to the military again. Today had been a great step forward so now she needed to see how the club would be.

The family drove out to the club and went inside. The host greeted them and showed them to a table. A minute later, the drinks waiter came around the got their orders of this. After a few minutes, the waiter came back to get their meal orders. Everyone ordered and sat talking some. Now would come the test. People in the club began dropping by and saying hi to the group. They all asked if there was something they could do for them. Fran was handling all this very well. She was now seeing that even with George gone, he would leave an excellent memory for everyone. This day really had been the turning point for Fran. She would always miss George but she now understood that her life was not ended, but pushing forward into zones for her that did not include George any more. She still had her parents and her children. She had a lot of life left to her if she didn't close herself up in a shell.

After their meal, the family left and drove back home. Fran now assumed her position as the head of her little family. They would require a lot of guidance from her and for now on. George Jr. had been talking with his granddad for a few past days. He was looking at entering the military academy at West Point. He was now assured his appointment there, as his father was a holder of the Congressional Medal of Honor award. Ted encouraged Jr., as he knew that George himself would have done. Jr. would be a sophomore in high school this next year. So his time was growing shorter and he wanted to get some planning in. Fran was just now learning of his plans. Her first reaction was fear that something might happen to him like his dad. Then she came around to understand that this would have been his father's wish also. Tracy would be in high school the year after next. She could

CHAPTER TWENTY SIX

have a whole life ahead of her. Maybe she could find a nice serviceman like she had. George would approve of this also, as well as Tracy's granddad. There really was a grand future for everyone left here for now.

A CROWN OF GLORY

CHAPTER TWENTY SIX

A CROWN OF GLORY